McAl…
AND C…
D…

Brevington demanded: 'Was that you doing that shooting?' Lawson admitted that it was and the colonel said: 'You damn fool. I had not yet decided that McAllister had to be killed.'

Lawson said: 'I make my own decisions. I decided long ago that I was going to rub McAllister out.'

Brevington nodded. 'I have made my decision now. McAllister will have to be killed. But we won't have you going off half-cock again, Lawson. Next time, we'll be organized. Done with the greatest precision and economy. One bullet, one dead man.'

Lawson showed his wolf-teeth.

'My pleasure,' he said.

Further McALLISTER Westerns in Hamlyn Paperbacks

McALLISTER ON THE COMANCHE CROSSING
McALLISTER AND THE SPANISH GOLD
McALLISTER NEVER SURRENDERS

McALLISTER AND CHEYENNE DEATH

Matt Chisholm

Hamlyn Paperbacks

McALLISTER
AND CHEYENNE
DEATH
0 600 20372 7

First published in Great Britain 1982
by Hamlyn Paperbacks

Hamlyn Paperbacks are published by
The Hamlyn Publishing Group Ltd,
Astronaut House,
Feltham,
Middlesex, England

Made and printed in Great Britain by
Cox & Wyman Ltd, Reading

1.

It was the year in which Milly McNickle had her first baby that the Indians came and camped on Howard Creek in the Black Horse Valley. McAllister always remembered it because Doc Robertson was unable to attend so McAllister had to deliver the child. A man is apt to remember that kind of a year.

There was the joshing for one thing, of course. How many times in their lives had folks ever heard of a man delivering a child? So McAllister came in for a lot of ribbing. He did not seem to care much; but when folks started *sending* for him to deliver a child, he thought it time to call a halt. He said if Doc Robertson promised not to raise horses, he would not play midwife any more.

He could duck out of a thing like that easily enough. To duck out of the subject of the Indians was another matter entirely.

The Indians were Cheyenne – part of the Northern Cheyenne who were affiliated, as you might say, to the Sioux Nations. It was a pretty small band of them with White Bull as their chief. At least that was what the white people called him. To McAllister, who knew his Cheyenne, he was an important man and certainly was chief among the small band who chose to follow him for the winter hunt. Only that year there was not much of a hunt, for the buffalo had failed to come, and Indian bellies were pretty hungry. No other game seemed to come either.

To begin at the beginning, McAllister was preparing for winter. In this high country it came early and it came hard. He started preparing in the fall when, in his opinion, the country was at its most beautiful. The birch along Howard Creek were all silver and russet browns and reds, splashed across with yellow. He worked on his big barn and his pens.

He had made up his mind to get his most valuable stock under cover this winter. He had cut hay all summer and spent his last dollar on corn. He reckoned he would get through this snow without losses. God willing.

It was Si Tallin who stopped off to be neighbourly and take a friendly drink and told McAllister about the Indians.

'I seen them a few days back, Rem. Must be twenty lodges, I reckon. Up here for the winter hunt. The folks ain't too damned pleased about it. I heard tell these're Cheyenne. Well, hell, the army's fightin' Cheyenne. All over. Maybe these ain't hostiles right this minute, but maybe they was a week back an' maybe they will be again come next week. Who knows with goddam Indians?'

They drank and Tallin made flattering remarks about McAllister's whisky, which usually meant he wanted more.

One fall such as this, long ago, old man Chadwick McAllister had dumped his son on the Cheyenne for a month while he went off hunting. The month had run into several years and old Chad he was pretty taken aback when he came to find that his son was a pretty good Indian, but could no longer pass for a whiteman. Now Chad was partial to Indians one way and another, but it did not seem right that a white boy should grow up an Indian. So he made McAllister's foster-father, Many Horses, some handsome presents and carried young Remington off to be reared in the brush country of Texas. Here he learnt the whiteman's lessons – to chew baccy, swear and drink whisky. He also learned a thing or two about women before his voice broke.

Chad's separation of Rem McAllister from the Indians had not been quite timely enough. He never forgot what Many Horses had told him and taught him, nor did he forget the warmth of the life in an Indian band, his close relations with other humans and the rectitude which every Indian child accepts without argument. In short, he had learned the Indian right and wrong. Chad tried every now and then to knock the Indian thoughts out of the boy's head, but he never really succeeded. If he had, this story would not have to be told.

He asked Tallin whose band it was on Howard Creek.

'Whose band?' Tallin said. 'Christ, how should I know whose band, man? They're Indians. I didn't ask 'em their goddam names.'

McAllister saddled his favourite horse, Oscar, and rode down the valley the following morning. He admitted to himself that the Indians' presence made him uneasy. If this band was not hostile, why wasn't it on the reservation? But if it was hostile why wasn't it out fighting the soldiers? He would know soon enough.

Tallin was right. There were some twenty tipis parked on the edge of the breaks not far from the creek. It was a nice spot. McAllister had his first cabin there when he came into this country. He could still see the burned remains of his cabin. Si Tallin had done that when he rode for Edward C. Larned, the cattle baron. Tallin had lived that down by proving to be a good neighbour. McAllister might never forget, but he forgave easily enough. Life was too short to bear grudges.

As soon as he rode into that Indian camp, he got the feel of it.

First, it was a worried camp. There were young men here who had lately been fighting the soldiers. He could not prove it, but he was pretty sure. Their faces were surly as they watched him come. The women were scared and they could not hide the fact. The old men were anxious. Their manner turned to wonder when they heard his fluent Cheyenne. They had never heard a whiteman speak their tongue this way before. Most likely many of them had never seen a whiteman this close before. He looked for guns and did not see any.

White Bull came out to greet him and it was then that McAllister, with his great memory for faces, recollected him. This was a cousin of Many Horses and not unlike the chief to look at. His hair had white in it now and he was stooped and faintly hesitant in manner. McAllister remembered him as a warrior in his prime. A handsome man with a marvellous air of confidence. They embraced and McAllister called him 'father', which pleased White Bull.

In the warmth of the tipi, leaning against their back-rests, the old man said: 'I remember you well, son. You were called the Diver.' He smiled at the memory. 'You could not swim until you were taught, but you could always dive. They were good days.'

They talked of this and that for a good while, as Indians did, politely and with care, avoiding offence. McAllister produced a little whisky. He wanted the old man to talk and to do so frankly. White Bull did not approve of whisky but he thought a little did no harm. Finally, they got around to the nub of the matter. Why were he and his band here?

White Bull said: 'Diver, you know that young men love to fight. It has always been so, therefore it is right. When there are many enemies, they like to fight more, which also is natural. The soldiers have come into our country and the game has been driven from our prairies. The gold-hunters have torn open the breast of our mother earth. Bad times have come and the young men think they can put it right by fighting. They have not yet learned that there are some fights which cannot be won. You and I know different, but they believe it and think that if they are brave enough and strong enough and if their medicine is good, they must be victorious. It is a little sad, I think. Do you agree?'

'Yes,' McAllister said, 'very sad.'

'The soldier chiefs say the young men are bad because they fight. I find this a strange reasoning and I cannot believe that the white chiefs mean what they say. Only a fool would talk that way. The young men fight for their people. What else is there for a young man to do? What else is a young man for? I am getting old and I think differently. The winter of my life approaches as also does the winter of the year. Cold and hunger temper a man's mind and his courage. Winter calls for a different mind and a different courage. Now I have to think how my band shall come through the winter. I have told the soldier chief at the fort that I took no part in the fighting with the soldiers. This is true. You believe me?'

'I believe you, father.'

'Good. The young men have come in and the Cheyenne nation has divided for the winter hunt. As you know, when the snow comes we scatter and in one and twos hunt the scarce game so that we may eat meat when the buffalo meat and the pemmican is gone. This year there have been few buffalo and the white hunters have disturbed the little game there is. The People are hungry. Through the winter, they will be hungrier. The young men will not fight in winter. They will hunt. Maybe in the spring when the grass is up and the ponies grow strong again, they will go out to fight the soldiers once more, but I hope not. Too many are dying and soon there will be no more young men to make our women with child. What will happen to the People then? I hope to keep the young men quiet. But the People are frightened and they are right to be frightened. How may the soldiers know those of us who do not want to fight? The young soldiers are strangers to us. They know nothing about us. Any Indian man, woman or child is a target for their guns. You know this, Diver.'

'I know it.'

'Then what shall we do to make ourselves safe from the soldiers?'

'Go close to the fort. I'll talk with the commanding officer there.'

'I have asked him already and the agent. The agent says come near, the soldier chief says that he will shoot us if we come near. The chief who is higher than him says this must be so.'

McAllister said: 'An American flag, father. You must put an American flag above your village so that the soldiers will know that you are peaceful.'

The older man nodded. 'This is good, but how shall I ask the soldier chief for one? If I go to the fort, he will shoot me.'

'I'll go to the fort. He'll listen to me.'

'Good.'

They talked on for an hour or more. When McAllister left the tipi, he talked with a few of the band with whom he had hunted in the past. Then he rode home along the valley, through the russet browns and yellows of the fall, and reached home before dark. The sky was clear and the air felt clean and sharp. No sign of snow yet, he thought, but it would be here soon. He hoped he had enough hay in for the winter. Lige Copley was forking hay in the barn. Lige was his only help at the moment. He was the son of a former slave who worked in Black Horse as a blacksmith. The boy was hard-working, intelligent and as devoted to horses as McAllister himself. A man and a boy were not enough for the work to be done and McAllister had hired Greg Talbot, a hill rancher, for the past year, but now Greg had gone back into the hills to run his own place.

When McAllister unsaddled Oscar in the barn, Lige said: 'There was a man here, boss, askin' for you.'

'Did he say who he was?'

'Nary a word. Seemed kind of tight-mouthed.'

'Did he say what he wanted me for?'

'No, sir. He was a saddle-bum by the looks of him, huntin' a job likely. One of them fifty-dollar-saddle ten-dollar-horse men.'

'Throw Oscar into the corral,' McAllister said. 'I'll cook us some chow.' Lige was the lousiest cook McAllister had ever met up with, which was saying something after years of experience with horrific trail cooks. He had allowed Lige to cook one meal since he first employed him and that had been one meal too much. It was now a joke between them, a kind of routine they went through daily. Lige thought the joke was terrific.

'You certain sure you don't have a notion to allow me to cook the meal, boss?'

'Certain sure, Lige. I still have a wish to live.'

Lige kept his face straight, but he shook with laughter. He said: 'Come on, you,' to Oscar and the horse followed him across the yard to the corral.

As he went into the house, McAllister looked at the sky. Still no sign of snow. He wondered who the man who had asked for him was. He threw some slices of bacon into the pan and heard the appetising sizzle. While he prepared the meal, he thought about the Indians down on Howard Creek. When he thought about them, he had an uneasy feeling in the pit of his stomach. He called that his Indian instinct and it was usually right. He had come to respect it. Maybe it was plain hunger.

When Lige came in, McAllister asked him if he had

washed his hands. 'Your ma told me to ask you that every time you come in to eat.' Lige went out to the pump and McAllister heard him pump up about one cupful of water. When Lige came in again, McAllister spooned bacon, potatoes and onions on to their plates, put the coffee pot on the table and said: 'Tomorrow we'll make bread, boy. I surely hunger for bread.'

'Me too,' said Lige.

'Lige.'

'Yessir.'

'We've got to find us another hand. There is more'n enough work here for two men.'

'We'll make out, boss.'

'All work and no play makes Jack a dull boy.'

'Playin's for kids,' Lige said.

They ate steadily, quickly and in silence as was the custom. They each saved a potato till the end, so they could mop up the grease with it. They reckoned that was the best part of the meal. Then they sat around to drink their coffee and McAllister filled his pipe. They both belched a couple of times and then they were ready for conversation. When they were both there, this was their habit. This was the boy's learning time and a time of great pleasure for McAllister. He had never known a boy that wanted to learn more than this one.

Lige was a tall gangling boy, too tall and too thin for his age. His mother had told McAllister: 'He outgrow his strength, Mr McAllister.' McAllister was of the opinion that there was no such thing as outgrowing your strength. Lige was merely at that stage when he needed physical work to build the muscle and food to fuel it. Each day he watched that boy tuck away twice as much chow as himself. The boy's capacity for food was a source of great wonder and admiration on his part.

'Lige,' he once asked, 'do you ever stop eating?'

'Sure, boss, when I sleeps.'

Lige had one of those black faces the eastern cartoonist used to make a meal of, exaggerating the lines till every whiteman who looked at it knew it as a symbol of the stupid, unlettered black man who was good for a laugh any time. But Lige was smart and he was dedicated. His body wasn't built for a horseman, but his brain was. He had that rare commodity – horse-sense, which was something that could not be taught. He understood horses and they understood him. He had never feared a horse and they knew it.

When they had washed the dishes, they went into the yard to look at the night. The stars were not in evidence. There was a damp, cold feel to the air.

'Lige, I have to ride to the fort tomorrow. I'll be gone maybe a couple of days. You reckon you can mind the store while I'm gone?'

'Sure.' As they turned back into the house, the boy said: 'Snow tonight.'

McAllister said: 'I reckon you're right at that.'

2.

The following morning, McAllister was up an hour before first light. It was cold with that deadly and sudden drop in temperature which told of snow about. When he looked out of the window, he saw a light dusting of snow along the valley. When he looked over at the ridge to the west, the trees were draped in gossamer white. It might look picturesque, but McAllister hated it. Winter to him had always meant hard times driving horses and cattle in a freezing temperature, hands and feet dead with cold, breaking the ice for water, floundering in drifts while trying to save cattle. As he thought about it, he told himself he should have stayed down in Arizona.

Lige came from his bunk, blue and shaking with cold. He looked the essence of misery.

McAllister said: 'If you don't like it, you should of stayed in Africa.'

'Africa, boss? My folks come from Alabama.'

'You keep moving now and keep warm. You go sick on me, boy, and your ma'll skin me.' He slung beans into a pot and bacon into the pan. He could use a mansize steak of beef this morning. 'And while I'm gone you see you eat, hear? I want to see you fat and sassy when I get back.'

Lige looked at him poker-faced and asked: 'You mean I ain't sassy enough?'

McAllister cooked enough bacon to make sandwiches. They were favourites of his. He didn't have any bread so he made biscuits. He also had some meat biscuit which he put into a saddlepocket – the ubiquitous jerky, two large handfuls. Tobacco. Peggin' strings. Powder and shot. Percussion caps. Anybody would think he was going to fight a war. Salt. Turn the bacon. He reckoned he'd fry some potatoes and some onions. With a full morning belly, he could last till tonight. He wondered why the hell he'd promised to go to the fort for old White Bull with the weather closing in this way. Though maybe heavy snow would not fall for a week or two. Still . . . he went to the window and looked along the valley . . . he'd hate to get caught out there in the hills in a blizzard. He would take the gelding, Oscar. He was the strongest and most intelligent of his horses.

He flicked the bacon from the pan on to plates and put the potatoes and onions in the hot fat.

'That sure smells good,' said Lige.

McAllister said: 'You don't realise it. You're living on the fat of the land.' Lige had McAllister's old Henry rifle down from its pegs on the wall and was cleaning it. He suggested that if McAllister spotted a mule-ear on the way home he might think about knocking it over. They could do with some deer-meat. McAllister said sure. He remembered the man who had come asking for him. If he returned . . . what should Lige tell him? He pondered. It could be ominous, a man coming here asking for him. He could be a part of McAllister's past, just out of the pen, feeling he owed McAllister something, like a bullet in the head. 'You tell him to go into town and see your pa. He'll know what to say to the man.'

Lige said: 'I remembered – he was a tall feller. He had red

hair and he could sure use a shave. His face was real white.' By that McAllister presumed he was pale. 'His horse was a sorrel and mighty stylish. You know . . . '

'How did he wear his gun?'

'Right side, butt forward.'

'Boots?'

'Not cowman's boots.' That meant they didn't have high heels.

'Spurs?'

'Nossir, he had a mighty handsome quirt.'

'Saddle?'

'California single-rig.'

'Hell,' said McAllister, 'I thought you looked at him with your eyes shut. What happened, you get your memory back in your sleep?'

'I thought about it last night. It seemed kind of important to you, so I thought about it. An' all come back.'

'How old?'

'I can't never tell how old white folks is.'

'Older than me?'

'Mebbe.'

'How did he call me?'

'Just McAllister, I guess. Aw, once he said the marshal.'

'He did, huh?'

'Yessir, he sure did.'

McAllister brought the two plates to the table and started to eat. He talked with his mouth full. 'I'm going to light out directly I'm through eating, Lige. You wash the dishes, then feed the horses. You're in charge. You reckon you can make out just like you and me're working together?'

'Sure.'

'Good. Don't get on an unbroken horse while I'm gone. You break a leg or an arm on your lonesome here, you could lie around for days. Just do the routine chores is all, hear?'

'Yessir.'

'Good man.'

Five minutes later, McAllister was tramping to the starve-out for Oscar, his saddlepockets slung over his shoulder, a gunny sack of corn to tie to his saddlehorn and his Henry in his hands. He dumped it all in the barn and whistled. Oscar was at the gate waiting for him when he reached the corral. McAllister opened the gate and the canelo walked out. As McAllister closed the gate, the cinnamon roan trotted into the barn. He knew he was for the saddle and he was eager to go. Lige came from the house to help McAllister with his gear. When he was all set to go, McAllister looked over the saddle at Lige and said: 'Lige, you have any bad problems, you ride and tell your daddy. The doctor or Dice Hoggart at the Belle of Union'll always give you a hand or advice.'

Lige said, opening his eyes wide, 'Don't you be anxious now, boss.'

'And Lige . . . '

'Yessir.'

'If you ride into town, you saddle Brownie. In fact, we'd better call Brownie your horse from here on.'

Lige looked slightly stunned. He said: 'You ain't tellin' me . . . Mr Mack, you ain't sayin' you're givin' me my own horse, for God's sakes?'

'That's what I'm telling you.'

'Jeez . . . '

'You earned him. You're a horseman so it's fitting you have a horse of your own.'

Lige was lost. He wandered out of the barn and stood looking across to the starve-out where Brownie stood with the other horses. McAllister led Oscar out into the yonder and stepped into the saddle. When he rode north along the edge of the creek, Lige was still standing in a daze.

The valley had an eerie and strange kind of loveliness that morning; the air was crisp and dry. A morning which made a man glad to be alive. Oscar stepped out briskly. His hooves cracked on the hard ground with a new sharp note.

A mile down the creek, McAllister found some of Si Tallin's longhorns which had drifted across the creek. He took fifteen minutes of his time to drive them back, as any neighbour would. He saw they were putting on tallow and were in good condition. One old mosshorn steer tried to evade him, but Oscar stayed with him and they turned the animal back across the water.

Pretty soon, as he went on, he saw the smoke from the Indian camp. He was sighted and White Bull was out to give him greeting. They exchanged no more than a few words and the Indian seemed well pleased that McAllister was on his way to the fort. As he rode on through the camp, McAllister took a good look at the younger men and he could not miss the fact that he received pretty sullen looks. He called greetings in Cheyenne to them, but they did not reply.

In a short while, he was riding through the breaks. Beyond the breaks, he was wending his way through a number of smaller, high valleys and in time came to Greg Talbot's place, almost inaccessible on a small shelf moated by a rushing mountain torrent. From there Greg could see anybody coming into his valley. He ran a few cattle, nursed a truck garden and hunted. He knew that Greg must be away from home or he would have hailed McAllister. Here McAllister hit a fairly well-established trail and once more Oscar hit his hammering, steady pace. The snow held off, but the sky was ominously dark and the cold was chilling. Halfway through the morning the cold drove McAllister to dismount and run beside the horse to keep warm. He came in sight of the fort late in the afternoon.

It stood alone in the wide circle which the logging parties had cut in the trees which had been felled for the construction of the fort. The country around looked bald and curiously vulnerable as a naked man or woman would be. As McAllister rode out into the open, he could see such a logging party winding its way from the northeast, wagons and mounted men moving slowly.

The fort itself had been constructed by army engineers and was composed almost entirely of logs – high walls surrounded it, inside which stood barracks for the soldiers, officers, officers' quarters, stables and store-houses. There were fire steps along the walls and he could see the small dark figures of the soldiers forever on the lookout for Indians. There had been men killed here during the summer and the army was still jumpy. Not for the first time, McAllister wondered why White Bull had led his band so far into the north-west. The Cheyenne hunting range was far south of this. Had the Cheyenne come up here because their own buffalo range was bare? There were a number of questions McAllister wished that he had been able to ask White Bull, but courtesy forbade him and he had no desire to lose the Indian's confidence. There was nothing about the situation that McAllister liked.

He was challenged at the gate of the fort and, when he asked to speak with the commanding officer, a young sergeant took him to the office block, reported to the orderly room sergeant and he was asked to wait.

An hour later, he was told that the colonel would see him. He was not in the best of moods when he was shown into the man's office. The commanding officer, he found, was a Major Robert Whitehouse, acting colonel: a small man with tired eyes and an attitude that the whole world was conspiring against him. McAllister could find some sympathy for this attitude because this man was probably dealing with an enemy whose tactics he did not fully understand, a hostile environment, soldiers whose desertion rate was high and a general who disapproved of him. The man was old enough to believe that he should by now have reached a senior command post.

He scarcely looked at McAllister when he shook hands with him.

'Well, what can I do for you, Mr – er – ?'

'McAllister.'

'McAllister.'

McAllister was not going to stand in front of anybody's desk while the fellow lolled at his ease. He sought a chair and pulled it up before the desk. The major watched him with disapproval. You could see from his eyes that he neither liked nor approved of civilians. He was no doubt here to protect civilian settlers, but that did not mean that he had to approve of them. They were encumbrances that got in the way of military duties.

'Major, I've just come from –'

'Colonel,' said the major. 'I'm a colonel.'

'All right, colonel. I've just come from the camp of White Bull down on Howard Creek. He tells me –'

'Who is this White Bull?'

'He's leader of a small band of about twenty lodges of the northern Cheyenne. He's camped at the north end of Black Horse Valley.'

'I never heard of him, but go ahead.'

'He tells me that you gave him permission to camp and guaranteed him protection.'

'You can't expect me to remember every Indian –'

'He wanted to speak with you, but is afraid to come to the fort in case he's fired on by the soldiers.'

'A very sensible Indian, if I may say so.'

'He wants to camp near the fort so that he will not be attacked by the army.'

'He must be out of his mind. I would no more have Indians camped near this fort than I would have them camped inside it. My God, I must be allowed to take elementary precautions for the safety of my command. If he's on Howard Creek, that's where he stays.'

'How can I guarantee him his safety?'

'You can't and, if I may be permitted to say so, sir, it's none of your business.'

'Bill Steiner, the agent, told him his safety would be guaranteed by the army,' McAllister said.

'If you mean Captain Steiner,' the major said, 'that's none of my responsibility.'

'The War Department is responsible for the Indians.'

'This man White Bull has a number of young men among his band who have been out with the hostiles, Mack . . . Mack . . . er . . . You're not talking to a man who doesn't have the facts at his fingertips, Mack . . . er . . . '

'We're dealing with men's lives here,' McAllister said. 'Women and children, too.'

The soldier looked weary. 'You sound like somebody from back east, man. I've been fighting goddam Indians since the end of the war. I'm sick to death of goddam Indians. Steiner may love the bastards, but I do not. I've seen what they've done to white women and children. Maybe you didn't.'

There were plenty of answers to that. McAllister had also seen what whitemen had done to Indian women and children. That kind of argument would get you nowhere.

'You're telling me that you wash your hands of these people?'

'I'm telling you I'm not interested. If White Bull wants me to guard over him, he should keep his young men from raiding and warring. So they've all come home to spend the winter with him. As soon as spring comes and the grass is up, the ponies'll be strong enough to work and those same young men will be cutting white throats again. Mister, you're wasting my time.'

McAllister rose.

'Mister,' he said, 'I reckon I'm wasting mine too. I can't talk with a man who don't see Indians as human beings. That's what the Cheyenne call themselves – the Human Beings.' He started for the door, but by the time he reached there, his conscience forced him to make one more try. 'I'm begging you: think again. If you give White Bull a guarantee, it could stop the young warriors going on the war-path again. You'd maybe save white lives.'

'I don't know what your trade is, McAllister,' the soldier said. 'But I suggest you attend to it and leave me to attend to mine.'

McAllister left the office. In the orderly room, the sergeant and a private stared at him stonily. He knew they'd been listening. Outside, the snow had started to fall. He walked across the parade ground to the sutler's and found few customers in there. The sulter he knew from way back. A man named Bill Evans who had traded liquor down in Kansas. He did not have two cents to rub together then, but he looked as if his fortune had improved. But trade was slack right now. The goddam commanding officer kept the men working all hours. He expected a winter attack and he wanted the fort completed in a hurry. The man standing at the bar drinking was Portugee Phillips. They knew each other and they shook hands. It was said that the man was a part South Sea Islander, but he looked much like a Sioux-white cross to McAllister. He was a good man, handy and with plenty of sand.They took a drink together. McAllister said that he didn't want to push his horse further that day and wanted a place to sleep.

Evans said Portugee was sleeping in a store-room. McAllister could share with him if he wanted. Sacks of corn made a pretty fair bed. No charge. McAllister thanked him and the general talk began. McAllister repeated his meeting with the brevet colonel. Portugee smiled.

'He ain't our kind of folks, Rem. He don't understand.' Phillips was working for the army; packing and acting as a courier. But there would be no riding soon. This snow would lie and would be hell on a horse. 'Was I you, Rem, I'd get out of here come first light or you'll be here all winter.' McAllister thought that good advice.

He learned about the local situation from both men. The Sioux were bunched east of there. No matter this wasn't their territory. Sure, there was a scattering of Cheyenne with them, though some had pulled out. The older and wiser men did not want any part of the campaign that was coming.

'My God,' said McAllister surprised, 'you're not telling me the Indians aim to fight through the winter?'

'I reckon so,' Portugee said. 'And they stand a good chance of winning this round. They're changing their tactics; they have good leaders. They won't win in the long run, but you can't tell 'em that. I've tried. Chiefs don't take good advice, whichever side they're on. You and me should be Indian commissioners, Rem. We'd have this piece of trouble settled in no time at all.'

McAllister opined: 'You can't settle this, Portugee. The whites want what the Indians have. The Indians won't settle for having sweet damn all.'

The talk ran on and then Evans offered them a meal. The talk continued over the meal and then both men retired for the night. In the store-room, they talked some more before they went to sleep.

'All you can do with old White Bull is have him pull back into the breaks, Rem,' was Portugee's advice.

'If I can make him go. His fighting men won't take to the idea. I have the feeling they'll come down the valley to my place and lift my horses. And maybe my hair too.'

'Would they do that to you? I always thought of you as close to the Cheyenne.'

'Times have changed, like you said. I'm white and that's enough.'

'I wish you luck.'

'I have a feeling I'm going to need it.'

3.

McAllister headed home at first light the following morning. Snow was now falling steadily. As he shook hands with Portugee Phillips on the edge of the parade ground and mounted, a logging party was leaving the fort. The soldiers looked miserably cold.

'See you in the spring maybe,' Phillips said.

'Sure.' McAllister swung into the saddle and lifted a hand in farewell. When he rode out through the gateway, he faced the onslaught of the wind and was nearly blinded by the wall of snow that hurled at him. He rounded the east wall of the fort and then turned south. The force of the wind now hit him from behind and he was thankful that he was moving ahead of the storm and not having to force Oscar into it. The horse went ahead strongly. He had eaten well of Evans' corn. A couple of hours later, McAllister ran almost headlong into a party of Indians. They were as wrapped up as he was against the cold, but he knew at once that they were Sioux. He cursed because he knew no more than a few words of their language. However, they did not leave him in any doubt that if he was not very smart he could consider himself their prisoner.

The McAllister luck had not quite deserted him. On the chance that one of them understood Cheyenne, he used the language and his words were heard by the one member of the party who belonged to that people. The man pushed his horse forward out of the bunch of Indians and said: 'How is it that you speak the language of the People so well?'

'I am Diver, son of Many Horses. I think I know you.'

'Yes, I am Two Smoke. Many Horses' daughter, Moon, is my wife.'

'It is some years since I saw you,' McAllister said. 'I see that you have become an important warrior.'

'That is true,' the Cheyenne agreed. 'Tell me, Diver, do you work for the army?'

'No. I have come from the fort. I went there to speak for White Bull who is camped near my home.'

One of the Sioux made an angry remark and Two Smoke returned it in kind and told McAllister: 'He wants to know why we are talking. I say: Go to White Bull and tell him to send his young men here. They should be fighting alongside the Sioux.'

McAllister nodded. 'I shall tell him this.'

'Good. Now go quickly before these thick-headed Sioux become unpleasant.'

They clasped hands and McAllister went on his way without a second bidding. The Sioux looked a little put out, even murderous, but when Two Smoke spoke to them, they permitted McAllister to pass. He kept Oscar at a good pace for the next hour or so. He hoped fervently that there would be no more such encounters.

It stopped snowing around noon and the wind dropped a little, for which he was thankful. He rested Oscar for a short while and then went on. He began to wonder if he would ever reach home. He had been a damned fool to set out from home at all. Drifts were deepening and at times Oscar was up to his belly in snow. Hell, thought McAllister, how he hated winter. He reckoned he would hate it a good deal more before he sat before his warm stove. He camped that night in a pine forest, crouched over a fire with Oscar standing by munching on his oats. McAllister hoped forlornly that he was headed in the right direction. He wondered if, in fact, he had been riding in a circle for the last hour or two. It had been known.

Dawn found him stiff and miserable. He made hot coffee and enlivened it with a little whisky. This gave him a lift for a short while. Oscar seemed fit. The snow was still hanging about in the dark sky above, but at least it was not falling, for which fact McAllister gave thanks.

The morning travel was haunted by his uncertainty of where he was. He had never travelled this way during snow and it made possibly familiar landmarks unrecognisable objects. He crossed a frozen creek and failed to identify it. This made him doubly nervous that he might be going in the wrong direction. Snow fell steadily to noon when it held off, but he could get no glimpse of the sun and so make a rough estimate of his location. The wind was his only guide. He assumed that it was still blowing from the north. If he was right, at least he was going south.

For long periods now drifts were so frequent and so deep that Oscar would progress for as much as an hour in great leaps to get over them. McAllister knew the horse, however strong he might be, could not keep that kind of travel up for long. Where it was possible, McAllister went ahead and broke trail for the animal.

Towards dusk, with the snow still holding off, McAllister thought he recognised the small valley he was in and after dark he saw a small light flickering. He headed towards this, fell into a deep drift with Oscar and took about an hour to get out, using his hands as shovels to move the snow. Once out, he found that the light had disappeared and wondered if he had imagined it. He went in the direction of where he calculated it had been and stumbled on to the surface of frozen water. In front of him was a sudden rise in the land. He thought he must be at Greg Talbot's place. He bellowed for Greg at the top of his lungs and after about fifteen minutes saw the moving light of a lantern. After a while, he saw that it was Greg Talbot who greeted him with some round and hearty curses for bringing a man out on a night like this.

'Go around by the trail,' Greg told him, 'and I'll meet you.'

An hour later, McAllister was warm from the hot stew Greg ladled into him. That night he thankfully slept snug and was up by first light to press on. He rode down through the breaks to the spot where the Indians had been camped, riding through a crisp and clear morning, clouds gone and a weak but cheering sun shining. He found the Indian encampment gone, all tracks covered by a white mantle of snow.

A number of thoughts came into his head and he did not like one of them. There was nothing he could do for the moment – White Bull had made his decision or his young men had made it for him and he had moved camp. Maybe he had gone out against the soldiers and maybe he hadn't. Whichever way, he might meet the same fate wherever he was. McAllister turned for home. Oscar knew exactly where he was and he perked up a good deal. The valley trail was not easy to travel along and soon McAllister was forced to walk and break trail for the horse. But the snow held off, which was a blessing. However, McAllister did not sight his own place until well past noon.

Lige Copley was busy clearing the snow between the house and the barn. He looked pretty happy at seeing McAllister again.

'Boss, I sure thought you was snowed in at the fort or somethin'. I am sure glad to see you.'

McAllister laughed and said: 'I'm pretty damn glad to see you too, Lige. How've you made out?'

'I made out all right, boss.'

In the barn, he said: 'Give Oscar a good rub down, Lige. Make a mash for him out of corn. He earned it.'

McAllister unsaddled and slung his gear over his shoulder.

Lige said: 'That man were here again, boss.'

McAllister turned and looked at Lige. The boy looked as if he held a memory of a scare.

'Did he tell you where he was heading?'

'Sure. He headed for the house, boss.'

'The house?'

'He plumb took possession.'

McAllister walked to the house. As he opened the door, the delicious smell of cooking hit him right in the nose and he loved it. He kicked the door shut with a heel and stood looking at the man who had his back to him. He was standing at the stove, stirring a pot with a wooden spoon.

When the man heard the door slam, he turned.

He was just as the boy had described him, only the boy had not mentioned the tired eyes.

McAllister said: 'The boy described you, but just the same I didn't think it was you.'

The man said: 'It's been a few years, Rem.'

'How many?'

'Ten or thereabouts.'

McAllister laid his gear down on the floor and took three paces across the room. The two of them shook hands. Then they stood and smiled a little at each other. McAllister said: 'I smell you can still cook.'

The other laughed. 'I ate just one of Lige's meals and that was more'n enough.'

'I know what you mean. Can a man ask what you're doing in this neck of the woods?'

'It's no great secret. Leastwise not from you.' McAllister peeled off his buffalo coat. 'You're the reason. Not just for old time's sake. Well, yes, maybe it is for old time's sake. I followed a man from Arizona.'

'Do you have a warrant?'

'No, sir. This is private – between you and me and the other feller.'

'What other fellow?'

'Dom Lawson.'

McAllister reached down for his saddlepockets, opened one and produced his flask of whisky. He offered it to the other who shook his head and said: 'I don't use it much, remember?'

McAllister smiled and said, 'I thought maybe you had become corrupted.' As the other was not drinking, he put the flask on a shelf.

'So Dom is looking for me?'

'That's about the size of it.'

'You came a long trail for an old friend, Jim.'

'You'd do the same for me.'

'Goes without saying.'

Jim turned back to the stove and continued to stir the pot placidly. He said: 'Holler for that boy of yours. Chow's just about ready.'

McAllister went to the door and bellowed: 'Lige – come and get it or we throw it away.'

A few minutes later an eager Lige appeared, rubbing his hands together and grinning widely. McAllister expected him to drool at any minute. McAllister said: 'Lige, I want you to meet James Hickok.'

That pinned the boy's feet to the floor. His eyes were wide. 'Boss, you mean this here . . . ? Wild Bill Hickok?' Lige had never come face-to-face with living history before. 'I was askin' myself why he didn't never take his guns off.'

Hickok shoot with laughter. He said: 'There's one or two occasions, Lige.'

When they sat at table, they concentrated on their eating. The stew was perfection. There were even dumplings in it. McAllister saw that both he and Lige were overeating disgustingly. He let his thoughts drift back to the time when he had first met Hickok, both of them young and just out of the war. Both war-weary, Hickok had been a strong Union man, and McAllister was a Texas boy who had gone into his first battle at the age of fourteen. There had been some trouble in the Kansas City area. But that was a long time ago. Most men would have forgotten, but not Hickok. He had the pride of a simple man and it made a code of behaviour for him. A man with a code was, in McAllister's book, a rung or two higher up the scale than a man without one. What McAllister had done to help him had, in his opinion, been trivial enough. But not trivial enough for Hickok to have forgotten it. There were times when men called Hickok's pride vanity and maybe sometimes it was, but his vanity was that of a man who did what he thought was right.

Lige did not take his eyes from Hickok all through the meal.

Afterwards, Lige washed the dishes while the two men sat around the stove and talked. Hickok had always liked talk. His speech was rough at times and his list of words was not a long one, but he spoke with a marvellous ease, making his stories come to vivid life for his listeners. When the dishes were done, Lige lay in his bunk, listening. After a while, he fell asleep and they could hear his snores.

Hickok said: 'I could have wrote, Rem, but it didn't seem quite the same. I didn't have nothin' on, so I thought I'd come up here an' have a look at the high country. The snow come a mite quicker than I reckoned on.'

'And Dom – where do you reckon he's at right now?'

'No idee, boy. Around here someplace, that's for sure. But I didn't see him in a month or more.'

McAllister smoked his pipe, Hickok puffed at a cigar. Hickok still wore his hair long. It had been fine hair and many a woman had envied it. It was one of his vanities and it was said that he took great care of it. He didn't mind his friends ribbing him about it, but he had been known to draw a gun on a man he didn't care for joshing him on the subject. Now its fine auburn colour was fading and the grey was showing in it. McAllister noticed that he frowned deeply whenever he focussed his eyes on an object, and knew that he was still having trouble with his sight. This must have been deeply worrying for a man in Hickok's position, a known gunfighter who had a reputation to defend. If he failed to defend it, he was as good as dead. There was always some fool around who wanted to gain that reputation for himself. A man like Hickok, McAllister thought, needed eyes in the back of his head. Maybe a man like himself wanted them there, too.

Hickok's own thoughts were on his sight. He said out of the blue: 'Maybe me coming here to warn you wasn't all thought for you, Rem. Some of it was pure selfishness. My eyes ain't been too good again lately. It could put a few years on my life getting out of circulation for a while.'

McAllister laughed. 'In that case, you'd best keep away from me, Jim.'

Hickok smiled. 'You can point the feller out you want shot, boy.' He put another couple of logs into the stove and shut its door with a clang. 'This goddam snow ain't helpin', I can tell you.'

'You know we could be snowed in here for a good few months, Jim.'

'Sure. I been snowed in before.'

'How're you for cash?'

'Played a couple of games of poker in Black Horse and made me a few dollars.'

'I could use a hand around here. I could pay you forty a month.'

'Can you hell,' said Hickok. 'This is winter. Why should you need a man in winter? You and the boy're enough for this place.'

'Do you know how many horses I have?'

Hickok grinned. 'Sure, I know. I counted 'em.'

'Did you count 'em out on the range?'

'No, I never thought of that.'

'Forty a month.'

Hickok said: 'Can you bear it?'

McAllister said: 'I've seen you with horses, Jim. You're a top hand. So it's settled.'

'Wa-al, I won't say I couldn't use the money.'

When it came time to turn in, Hickok took the top bunk and McAllister the lower. The cold was already starting to creep into the house, so all they took off was their coats and boots. They put their buffalo coats over their blankets.

McAllister said: 'Do you still talk in your sleep, Jim?'

'So the ladies tell me.'

McAllister blew out the light. Lige's snores still filled the place and Hickok said: 'That kid snores the finest tenor I ever heard. Do the horses ever complain?' There was a long silence and McAllister thought his old friend had fallen asleep, but softly Hickok said: 'Maybe I made it sound simple, Rem. About Dom Lawson, I mean. It ain't quite that simple. You see he has Charlie Honniger and Vince Dufay along with him.'

McAllister was impressed. Unpleasantly so. He said: 'That sure complicates things, Jim,'

'It do at that. Still, sufficient unto the day an' all that. Night, Rem.'

'Night, Jim.'

Honniger and Dufay. Both of them executioners. But for Hickok, he would be as good as dead.

4.

Over one hundred miles away to the east, camped in the snow, were two hundred and fifty soldiers under the command of one, Colonel Arnold Brevington. They were volunteers to a man: store clerks, farmers' sons, cowhands – think of any trade or profession to which a young man could belong and it was represented. All of them ninety-day volunteers.

'Ninety days, gentlemen,' said the colonel, 'which means that we do not have too many left before we can attain glory, before we can fulfil our own personal manifest destiny.'

He sat on his camp chair behind his camp table. His officers sat on the ground, bent forwards to the slope of the tent walls, all cramped and uncomfortable, but all grateful to be out of the chilling wind of the high country winter. Most of them thought the colonel must be out of his head not to turn back. More of them would die out here from the accursed cold than would fall to an Indian arrow or bullet.

For a fruitless week now they had been following the band of Sioux which the colonel claimed was under the command of the up-and-coming chief Running Horse. This man had refused to come in at the command of the United States army and retire to the relative safety of the reservation, but had chosen the almost hopeless alternative of continuing the fight against the white invader. One point was in his favour. He had no women and children with him and he travelled light and fast; too fast for a regiment of volunteer cavalry.

Colonel Brevington, like a good hound, had sniffed at Running Horse's trail and, once having done so, was reluctant to give up the hunt. The thought of returning to base without killing a single Indian filled him with uneasiness and shame.

Major Leonard Newton said: 'Colonel, I would sure like to hear from you something concerning the men.'

Newton was second-in-command of the volunteers. In appearance, he was curiously like his commanding officer – medium height, stout and red-faced, getting just a little too old for the game he was engaged in. He had risen to the rank of lieutenant in an infantry regiment of the Union army in the latter part of the Civil War. He had liked the idea of being a soldier, but he had not been greatly enamoured of the facts of the soldier's life. He was, he knew and hated to admit the fact to himself, too damned sensitive for so bloody and violent a profession. Yet he was a man who did not like to fail himself nor to fail to live up to his wife's opinion of him. If civilization on the frontier was threatened by the savages, it was his duty to defend his own kind. If necessary, he should be willing to lay down his life while doing so. At this moment, he was physically very tired and wondering how much longer he could suffer the increasing cold and the unaccustomed hardship of staying in the saddle hour after hour and day after day. He was becoming increasingly fearful that he was on the brink of total failure.

Now he saw the colonel's angry eyes turn to him. He knew why the colonel was angry and he knew that the man despised and even disliked him. He was more than a little afraid of his superior, and was getting near to the time when he would admit the fact to himself.

The colonel said: 'Something concerning the men, huh? I'm sure you would, major. I have a pretty clear recollection of touching on the subject yesterday. You mean you don't recollect that, major?'

'I recollect it, colonel.'

'Then you will also recollect that at the time I said that we would discuss the subject some other time. I give you the same answer now.'

Newton steeled himself. He could feel that every officer there was watching him.

'Maybe we could consider this to be some other time, sir.'

The colonel bridled. He would have come back with some smart remark, but the ageing captain, Harry Brigg, said: 'We sure have to discuss the men, colonel, and that's a fact. The whole of this enterprise depends on the men, don't it?'

Brevington twisted his thick neck to glare at Brigg. This veteran ex-regular commanded more respect in him than his second-in-command, so he quickly switched his attention back to the major. If he could wither him, he might shut the captain up.

'I have nothing further to say about the men, major,' he said, 'except that from here on in we shall have to tighten discipline. I have noticed too much familiarity between officers and men. This must stop *instanta*, gentlemen. I do not intend to command a sloppy regiment. Do I make myself clear?'

Captain Brigg said: 'That ain't a regular unit, colonel, and no amount of talk will make it so. Every man and officer knows each other as civilians.'

'That being so,' said young Lieutenant James Lawrence, 'us officers hear a lot of truths regular army officers would never here. Which, to my mind, can only be good.'

The colonel snapped: 'Nobody is very interested in what a junior lieutenant has to say, mister. I suggest you sit still and listen to your superiors and learn a thing or two.'

In civilian life young Lawrence's father owned the bank. He also had large cattle interests, and his bank was owed a good deal of money by the colonel. Young Lawrence was a boy of some confidence and he had not been brought up to truckle to superior officers.

'You call us here for a council, Mr Brevington . . . ah . . . colonel . . . I guess us junior officers have as much a stake in this affair as anybody. Maybe the major and the captain don't have a notion to talk plain, but I do, sir. Every damn one of us knows –'

The colonel half-rose in his chair, threateningly. 'You speak when you're spoken to, mister. I'll have discipline here.'

Major Newton screwed up his courage, shamed by young Lawrence's frankness.

'Colonel,' he said, 'the boy's right.'

'What!'

'What every one of us knows is that the men don't have more than another day in them. You can't push volunteers like we're pushing these boys.'

'I can't? Who in God's name are you telling he can't? We have come out to fight Indians, sir, and I shall not return to base until I have fought some. What has happened to the manhood of this nation?'

'The terms of their engagement clearly state –'

'To hell with the terms of their engagement,' the colonel shouted. 'If I order the advance to continue, it shall continue. Any man speaking against my orders, any man threatening to turn back will be guilty of mutiny and I know how to deal with mutineers.'

Captain Harry Brigg said quietly: 'That's kind of wild talk, colonel. I guess we could have done without that being said.'

The colonel was on his feet.

'Don't you dare, sir . . .'

The major tried to cool the situation.

'Colonel, we all admire you for your tenacity. We're all here to fight Indians. It's just we're all trying to face the reality of the situation which is that if we push the men much further through this kind of weather, we ain't going to have any men.'

'And where will they go? I tell you, these fellows are entirely dependent on their officers. If they're handled firmly, they will respond accordingly. We must keep them to their duty. That's what we're here for.'

The major said: 'Maybe they're entirely dependent on us, colonel, but that's not saying so much. We're lost and they know we're lost.'

The colonel sat down again and glowered at them, his small eyes going balefully from one face to another.

Finally, he said, as if to convince himself as much as them: 'We are suffering from a temporary loss of location, nothing more. You know as well as I do that this can happen in this kind of country and this kind of weather.'

The major said: 'In this kind of country and weather it isn't so damned temporary.' He was astonished at his own bravery right under the colonel's intimidating eyes.

The colonel said: 'I have witnessed here tonight the most shameful exhibition of cowardice and irresolution that I ever thought to.'

Absolute silence met this statement. Eyes and faces were stony. For a very brief moment, the colonel looked abashed at what he had said. Then he worked up his anger again.

'I think it best,' he said, 'to ignore what has been said. I never thought to be ashamed of the officers of this regiment. We'll forget this ever happened. You're dismissed, gentlemen.'

The officers stared at him, then they slowly rose to their feet. They started to file out of the tent. The major was in the lead. However, when he walked out into the cold, he stopped so abruptly that Captain Brigg behind him cannoned into him. The captain heard his superior say to himself in a kind of exasperation: 'Jesus, I'm second-in-command of this outfit. I'll be goddammed if I let him get away with it.'

The captain said: 'Good for you, Len,' and slapped him on the shoulder. The major seemed unaware of his presence. The faint light from the tent touched his rubicund face. His rather weak mouth was set in a determined grin of anger. He waited until the others had left the tent and then stooped to enter again.

The colonel's back was to him. He heard the clink of bottle on glass and knew the man was pouring himself a drink.

'Arnold,' he said, 'I think we should talk this thing out.'

The colonel swung around on him. Some liquor slopped from the glass. Brevington's face was furious.

'You think what?'

'I think we should talk this out.'

'Then you have another think coming to you, Newton. I do not discuss such matters with officers whose guts have run out on them.'

Newton fought to control his own outrage.

'That is the second time that you have personally insulted me.' he said. 'I must ask you to apologise and retract.'

The colonel hurled the whisky down his throat and clenched his teeth on the fire of the liquor. He gave a great gasp and shudder before he said: 'You get the hell out of here. Don't use my given name to me, mister. Another word out of you and I'll put you under arrest and strip you of your rank. Do I make myself clear?'

'I think,' said Newton, amazed that he could outwardly stay so calm, 'that you are losing your senses, man. The failure of this mission has been too much for you. You should be concentrating your mind on how we are going to get the regiment alive back to base. You cannot silence me. I have every right as second-in-command to offer my advice.'

The colonel sneered: 'All right – you've offered your goddam advice and I have rejected it. Now clear out. I apparently have a lily-livered second-in-command and must take the total responsibility for the regiment on my own shoulders.'

'Will you listen to me, man?' Newton found his fury breaking out and taking control of him. 'Don't you realize that when we get back to civilization I shall submit my report on this whole sorry business. I am a respected member of the community. Nobody could ignore a report from me.'

'Who will listen to a report from an officer in disgrace, brought back under arrest for mutiny and cowardice?'

'All I ask, Brevington, is for you to remember that you hold the lives of two hundred and fifty men in your hands.' He turned and went out of the tent into the cold night. Outside he paused, still shaking with rage and frustration. As he stumbled through the snow back to his own bivouac tent, a sense of utter foreboding came over him, not so much for himself, but for the men for whom he was responsible.

My God, he thought, I know their families, their wives and sweethearts. How can I tell a mother and father that their boy was lost because of that fool's megalomania?

A man approached him in the gloom. He saw that it was the bulky figure of the sergeant, Ivor Drewsky. The man was a blacksmith by trade. He had seen years of service in the regular army and the volunteers.

'Sir.'

'What is it, Ivor?'

'Just wondered if you heard anything, sir.'

'Such as?'

'Are we turning back.'

'I don't think so.'

'We're lost, ain't we, major?'

The major smiled and said: 'The phrase is that we are suffering a temporary loss of location, sergeant.'

'Aw, Christ,' said Drewsky. 'Major, you and me both know the men can't hold up much longer.'

The major said: 'The way I see it, Ivor, is it's up to men like you and me to hold 'em up.'

'Easy said, sir.'

'But we'll do it, sergeant.'

He turned away and crawled into the little tent. The cold was increasing. He took a nip from his whisky bottle and drew his buffalo robe over him. His last thought as he dropped off into an uneasy sleep was made out loud: 'Where in hell does this end?'

5.

Great events either grow out of small incidents, which may seem insignificant at the time, or are made up of them.

So far as McAllister was concerned, the next few days were filled with the everyday urgencies of his life as a raiser of good horses. He had so far during his first years as a horse breeder followed the local custom of leaving part of his horse-band out on the range to fend for themselves through the bitterly hard months of winter. He had never been too happy with this arrangement. He would agree that winter was a great sorter-out of weak stock. Those which survived must be tough, for during the worst weeks, the animals, no longer able to paw through the hardening snow to the poor grass beneath, were reduced to eating twigs and the bark of trees. Thus did the horse-herds of the Indians make out. However, he was convinced that, in the long run, the experience of winter on the range did not do his stock any good. This winter, he was determined to have his animals nearer to hand so that he could fork them some winter feed.

Hickok and he, with young Lige to aid them, spent two hard days gathering horses and driving them towards the home place, throwing them into a large pen which lay on ground slightly sheltered against the elements by higher ground. At the end of the two days, during which the weather had turned worse and the cold increased, they retired to the warmth of the cabin with some relief, thankful to once more have a hot meal inside them and a stove to drive the cold from their bones.

McAllister laughed and said: 'Changed your mind about saving my life, Jim?'

Hickok groaned and said: 'If I had of knowed . . .' He must have noticed some subtle reservation in McAllister's manner. 'Something wrong, Rem?'

Flipping bacon in the pan at the stove, McAllister said: 'Now you ask – yes. There's a colt missing.'

'And you don't reckon he died on you?'

'I reckon not. Well, it's not likely. Younger and weaker animals than him are all right. And you know as well as I do a colt don't go off and quit his bunch, not any time and certainly not in this kind of weather.'

'Who'd go in for lifting horses this time of the year?'

'Depends on the horses, Jim. This colt is a real beauty. Called him Caesar. I have his fillies all marked out in my mind for him. He's mostly California canelo with some pure mustang and quarter horse in him. He looks good and he is good. Acceleration and plenty of bottom. A stopper and starter and an all-day horse. I ain't really pushed him yet. I was going to do that in the spring.'

They ate their meal in silence and, while Lige washed the dishes, the two men enjoyed their pipes. Hickok was smoking some of McAllister's black and unmentionable weed.

He said: 'Jesus, Rem, this tastes like shredded horse-shit with a mite of camel throwed in.'

McAllister said: 'It sorts the men from the boys.'

'More like the inhuman from the human. Rem, I been thinking about this here colt of yourn. You thinking what I'm thinking?'

'Maybe. Dom Lawson was always horse-crazy. I never knew a villain who knew horses better or who fancied other men's more.'

'One of your own horses would sure be certain sure bait for you.'

'How do I track a horse in this weather?'

'True. But I reckon old Dom knows just what you're going to think next.'

'What's that?'

'Wa-al, if you can't track a horse what do you do?'

'I calculate which way a horse-thief would head and I go take a look there.'

'Right. So what do you do?'

McAllister smiled. 'You make me sound like a damn fool, Jim, but I do just that. I go look.'

'Where at?'

'The breaks.'

'Let's head that way in the morning.'

Lige swung around from his dishes. 'You'll need me along, boss.'

'Like hell we'll need you along, boy. You stay and mind the store.'

'I hear you tell my daddy you was going to teach me all there was to know about this here horse business.'

Hickok said, grave-faced: 'You take that kind of sass from your hands, Rem?'

McAllister grinned: 'You're a regular little old fire-eater, ain't you, Lige?'

Lige was not too sure how to take that, but he said, nodding his head with some vigour: 'I sure is, boss.'

6.

The three riders halted as the weak midday sun tried to fight its way through the lowering clouds. Then they saw the smoke from the cabin's stone chimney. They had spotted the place on the way into the main valley a week before. They did not know the name of the man who lived there. They neither needed to nor wished to. The place was ideal for their needs. Remote. In winter, with the snow lying, nobody would come near the place for months maybe. They did not want months. A week at the outside would see their chore through, they thought.

Dom Lawson was leading the young stallion. He glanced back at it now, admiring, never more pleased with a horse. It had all the characteristics of a good canelo plus the sturdiness of a good quarter-horse. Just the way it stood, you could see how alert and full of vigour he was. Dom liked a horse with some fire in its belly and this nag had plenty.

Dom himself was a strange mixture of a man. He was on the small side, wiry and tough. He was an almost unlettered man, but intelligent. He possessed so many skills that it was a puzzle to know why he did not use them legitimately. He was an expert cowman and could have earned good wages as a top-hand. Nobody knew and understood horses better. If he loved anything in this world it was horses. It was certainly not his fellow humans – though nobody could have accused him of disloyalty to a partner. When his word was given, it was usually good. With horses he had that marvellous firm gentleness that is the trademark of a good horseman. He could quieten a wild horse with his presence and tame one with his hands and voice. He was, anybody who knew him would admit, a magician with horses. With women, he was not so successful, for they sensed some latent cruelty in him towards them which they feared. That he possessed those secret ingredients which convinced his fellow-men of the strength of his character, not even his enemies would deny. And they were many. He did not possess the will to please. The need to arouse admiration and liking in his fellows he would have regarded as effeminate and a thing to be despised. He hated weakness of any kind, whether it was physical or mental. Dom Lawson was a hard man and he had never had to work at it.

Now, he said in that softly grating voice of his: 'The old bastard is home. Let's move in, boys.'

He gently urged his horse forward and the animal picked its way through the deep snow. It was a tall sorrel showing thoroughbred lines. Dom had stolen it from a wealthy rancher down in the Big Bend country. His gear was unadorned, but good, with the double rig of the Texan. But he was no Texan. He had come off an Ohio farm thirty years before. He had come very quickly because he had driven a six-inch blade into the belly of a local county sheriff. He was sixteen years old at the time and, so far as crime was concerned, he had never once looked back. From there he went on to bigger and worse things.

Riding behind him, Charlie Honniger said: 'Do we rub him out, Dom?'

Lawson replied: 'Not till I say. I'll size the situation up.'

As they rode towards the cabin on the hill, they came to deep drifts and were forced to dismount so that Charlie could go ahead and pack snow for the animals. Charlie did not like the job and he started cursing. They worked their way to a frozen creek which surrounded the hill like a moat and then started with some difficulty up the steep slope. Now Vince Dufay was cursing too. Lawson did not utter a sound. It was not in his nature to.

When at last they had fought their way to the top of the slope, there was old Greg Talbot outside his cabin and with his Remington rifle in his hands. He was no more than fifty paces from them and he could have picked any one of them off with case – as not one of them failed to see

'All right,' Greg sang out, 'that'll be far enough.'

Take a short look at Greg Talbot. I have described him

elsewhere, so we will not go into great detail. Let us just say that he was a life-long bachelor and it was easy to see why. No self-respecting woman would come near him. Maybe no woman who did not respect herself either. Even men shunned him – he did not have nice personal habits. He was long-haired, unclean and short on temper. There was nothing much about him that could be loved, in fact. To get down-wind of him was to suffer a stench that was not easily forgotten.

Be that as it may, he had stood by McAllister more than once in a tight spot. Because, mean though he was, he never forgot what he owed and he owed McAllister. Once he had saved McAllister's life – which somehow gave him a proprietory interest in the man. Greg was intractable, aggressive and gloomy. There was not much he feared on this earth and he was a crack shot with a rifle.

Unfortunately for one of the trio, none of them knew Talbot. It might have saved them some grief if they did. To them he was just another hill-nutty who lived on his lonesome.

To his partners, Lawson said: 'Leave the talking to me.'

He took a few paces in front of the others and said: 'Name's Bill Hardy.' Bill Hardy was a man he had killed five years before in Kansas. 'These here are my partners – Smith and Shaw.'

'What do you want?'

'McAllister sent us.'

'I don't give a monkey's fornication if the archangel Gabriel sent you. I asked you what you wanted.'

'We want to talk. We talked with McAllister and he told us you was the best man around here to talk with.'

'About what?'

'I don't aim to holler it at the top of my voice out here,' Lawson said. 'How about us coming in there?'

'Like hell you do. And what the hell're you doing with one of McAllister's horses?'

'He loaned it to me.'

'Like hell he did. That's a prize stud.'

Behind Lawson, Dufay said: 'Aw, for crissake, let me rub

the old fool out.'

Lawson said: 'Go ahead. But get off to the right. Maybe he can use that gun.'

As Dufay started to edge off to the right, old Greg bellowed out: 'You stay where you're at, or I drop you.'

While Talbot's eyes were on Dufay, the other man, Honniger, called: 'There's cash money in this for you, old man.'

Talbot flicked his gaze to Honniger and Dufay made his move. His gun was strapped on the outside of his buffalo coat, but encumbered with clothing as he was, the man was not as quick as he might be. Without apparent hurry, Talbot fired from the hip.

Dufay said: 'Aw, my Gawd.'

His right leg seemed to fly out from under him and to whirl around like an object independent of him. He fell into the snow.

Talbot, realizing with the shock of fright that the old single-shot rifle was now empty, backed to the door of his cabin in alarm, but before he could reach the cover of the building, Lawson and Honniger had drawn their guns and fired.

The force of the two bullets drove the man backwards, slamming his spine against the jamb of the doorway. His momentum turned him around the jamb and he fell into the cabin on his face.

The horses were jumping around and acting up. The young stud nearly tore himself free from Lawson's grasp. Lawson steadied the animal with a word and looked down at Dufay as he floundered around in the snow, his gun dropped, both hands gripping his thigh. The man's eyes showed his shock.

Lawson said: 'You could get yourself killed making a mistake like that.'

'The bastard,' Dufay said through his teeth. 'Oh, the goddam bastard.'

Honniger ground-hitched his horse and strolled easily to the cabin door, smoking gun in hand, to peer inside. He called back over his shoulder: 'Dead as mutton.'

He stepped inside and made a closer inspection of the dead man out of professional interest. He reckoned it was his own shot which had taken the old man in the heart. It would be Lawson's which had caught him in the head. Dom always went for the head. It was the more difficult shot and showed a wonderful confidence which aroused Honniger's admiration and envy.

He walked back to Lawson and said: 'You got him plumb through the head, Dom.'

'I know,' Lawson said. 'That's where I aimed.'

Together, they carried their fallen partner into the cabin, stepping over the dead man, and laid him on the only bunk in the place.

'Jesus,' Lawson said, 'this place stinks.'

'The old man stinks like a goddam polecat. I don't much like the idea of holing up in this, Dom.'

'Me neither, but I don't see we have much choice.'

From the bunk, Dufay said weakly: 'You two going to gab all day or do you fix this leg for me before I bleed to death.'

'You made the mistake,' said Lawson. 'Go ahead with some self-help, man. Use your scarf for a tourniquet.'

Dufay stared at him in amazement.

'You mean you – ?'

'That's what I mean,' Lawson said, no feeling one way or the other in his voice. 'We have to fix the horses up. We'll get around to you in good time.' He turned and looked down at the dead man and said to Honniger. 'Tote the old man out of here. Get him out of sight.'

While Honniger attended to the dead man, Lawson walked around the cabin, seeing how the old man's own animals were housed. There was a shed off to one side of the place with a small corral. There was a saddle-horse in the shed and some hay. There was room for one more horse in there. That would be McAllister's stud. He took a look at the pen and saw that it backed on to a wall of almost sheer rock. He did not like the idea of the horses being thrown in there. Anybody who came here and knew the dead man would spot something was wrong. He walked along one side of the corral and saw that there was a break in the rock there. He tramped through the snow and found that the break was large enough to hold the horses. Some brush thrown across the mouth of the break would hold them.

He walked back to the cabin and bawled out for Honniger to get a move on, he needed him. From inside the cabin, Dufay called in a shaking voice for somebody to come and help him. Lawson ignored the cry for help. He had tended himself often enough when he had been hit; it would not hurt Dufay to do the same.

He started unsaddling the horses and put the canelo into the shed. When Honniger appeared from the rear of the cabin, Lawson told him to throw the remaining horses into the break and to seal off its mouth with brush. Then he was to take them some hay from the shed.

He walked into the cabin and thought now that the old man had been removed, the place smelled just one degree better. Which was not saying much. Dufay was in real pain now, because the shock of the hit was starting to wear off.

Lawson said: 'I sure hope you don't have a notion to lay around for too long, Vince – I was banking on you being cook. I sure hate Charlie's cooking.

Towards dark, Dufay fell asleep and the other two thought they would enjoy some relief from his complaints, but they did not, because he continued to groan noisily. It started to snow again. This alarmed Honniger a little.

'Snow, Dom,' he said. 'Our tracks'll be covered. How does McAllister walk into our trap now?'

'If there was tracks,' Lawson told him, 'he would think he was following three fools or that we'd laid a trap for him. The snow suits us fine. He'll find us, all right. That son-of-a-bitch could find a black cat in the dark. Maybe now he won't suspicion a trap.'

'By God,' Honniger said, 'I hope you're right.'

He had encountered McAllister some years before in Crewsville, Arizona, when McAllister was marshal there. The experience had left an indelible scar on his memory. It had also left a scar along his lower left ribs where he'd been hit by a bullet from McAllister's gun.

7.

When McAllister and Hickok reached the spot at the far end of the valley where the Indians had first camped, they reined in and surveyed the white scene before them. The breaks lay off to the west, the bleak walls of sheer rock showing dark against the pale snow. The snow coming down on them whispered softly. The flow of the creek had stopped and its surface was like glass. McAllister looked back and saw that their trail in was even now almost covered. Both he and his companion had the same thing in mind – if they went on, would they be able to return?

Speaking for himself, McAllister knew he would go on. Even if it had to be done on foot, he would go on. He would have done it for any horse. For Caesar he would have gone barefoot. Horse-fever is a disease that leaves you far from sane, some men said. And maybe they were not far wrong. A part of McAllister's brain told him that he was a damn fool to do this for a horse. The world was full of horses.

But this, he told himself, was *his* horse.

Not only that – it was too good a horse to be in the hands of a thief. To McAllister's mind, there was nothing lower than a horse-thief. A man who stole cows was somebody who took part in a dangerous but eternal game. The man who stole a horse was a man who broke the first law. Sometimes, McAllister thought it was the only law that men in the West all took heed of. Even the men who broke it respected it in their way. They all knew the enormity of their crime. To them it was the ultimate gamble. Every horse-thief expected one day to have his neck stretched . . . by the law, by an owner, by any interested party who hated a horse-thief more than he hated the devil. This was a land of great distances in which a horse could be a matter of life or death. Often if you took a man's horse you condemned him to death. A man afoot was the potential victim of distance, thirst, hunger, wild beasts and wild Indians. He was not even safe from branded cattle to which a man afoot was no more than a natural target for their horns.

Hickok jerked his head at the west.

'Them the breaks?'

'Yes. That's the way my horse went. If we follow, we're sitting ducks.'

'Is there another way in?'

'From the west and from the north.'

'We could be sitting ducks from any direction.'

'True,' McAllister agreed. 'But we can take a look from above.'

Hickok jumped his horse nearer to McAllister. Both men were now covered with snow and looked like phantoms. Hickok said: 'You're hesitating, Rem. I reckon you think this is going to be a real bad business.'

'It has to be.'

'So you're wondering if you should lead me into it.'

McAllister smiled. 'That's about the size of it.'

'Aw, for crissakes,' Hickok said. 'I'm getting rusty, sitting around. Give a man a break.'

McAllister said: 'A few miles into the breaks, a man who worked for me called Greg Talbot has a cabin. That's the first place the rustlers would see. They couldn't miss it. I have a notion we should take a look at old Greg's place.'

'What sort of an hombre is this Greg?'

'Salty as all get out. I was never sided by a better man. But don't get down wind of him. He stinks worse than an old buffalo hide.'

Hickok laughed. McAllister led the way north, taking them slowly into the foothills where the drifts of snow became progressively deeper. Here there was some protection from the wind, however, and the horses were more willing to try. It was not long before the men had to dismount and McAllister broke trail. Three hours later, they were on a small plateau with the hills rearing above them on all sides except the south. Up here they suffered badly from the wind once more. The snow fell almost parallel to the ground. The horses hated it and wanted to drift before it.

When they halted, McAllister pointed south. Hickok found himself looking down a break which, so far as he could see, led to a large, shallow canyon. But visibility was bad and he could not be sure of what he saw.

With his mouth close to the other's ear, McAllister said: 'Can you see the cabin?' Hickok stared and stared through the veil of falling snow and could make nothing out. 'There – do you see that wisp of smoke?'

'I'll take your word for it,' Hickok said.

McAllister remembered the trouble the gunfighter was having with his eyes. He said: 'There's some shelter north of here, Jim. I'll lead you to it and we'll build a fire. Nobody's going to spot smoke in this. Then I'll take a look-see while you make some hot coffee.'

Hickok grinned. 'Sounds like a good idea.'

McAllister now led the way on foot slowly into the north. Both men hunched into the wind as it howled into their faces across the open ground. Inside a half-hour, however, McAllister led them into the shelter of a great cliff, the top of which went from Hickok's poor sight. Here they came into a cave, bringing their horses into cover with them. Magically, their hearing seemed to be restored to them. McAllister found wood for fuel within a short distance. He found punk and tinder. Hickok reckoned he had been here often. Soon they had a hot blaze going and they started to steam. While McAllister worked on the fire, Hickok attended to the horses, unsaddling them and giving them a brisk rub down. When he fed them, McAllister poured a little whisky into their oats. Then the two men each had a pull at the bottle.

Hickok said: 'I like a man who comes prepared.'

McAllister now said: 'I won't wait for coffee, Jim. I want to get there and back before dark.'

'Go ahead.'

McAllister pulled his Henry rifle from its boot and filled his pockets with shells from his saddlepockets.

Hickock watched him and then said: 'Don't start a war without me, Rem.'

McAllister said: 'Bank on it.' Then he walked out into the snow.

8.

His name was Mustang Jack Smithers and he had been hired by the army as a noted guide and Indian-fighter. Nobody was too sure how noted he was or what he was supposed to be noted for. One thing was certain – he did not know one Indian from another. He could not tell a Blackfoot from a Crow, or a Sioux from a Cheyenne. He was heard frequently to say that the only good Indian was a dead Indian. That seemed, somehow, enough to prove him bona fide.

He was not too bad at tracking animals and men, but so far he seemed a little short on common-sense and courage. No matter – his appointment as scout seemed fairly secure. Colonel Brevington had hired him personally and could not very well fire him for inadequacy.

Let it be said in Mustang's favour that he was the one to first discover the house.

'A goddam blizzard can't stop ole Mustang finding what he has a notion to find,' he said modestly later.

He had found the house by riding blindly into it and nearly breaking his horse's neck. 'Well,' he explained to himself, 'how's a man to see in all this damn snow?' Having ridden into the house, he was smart enough to right about turn and get back to the trudging column of troops before anybody else could ride into the house and nearly break their horse's neck.

'Colonel, sir,' he reported to Brevington, 'I have located a civilian dwelling. Trust ole Mustang to git you through.'

'What kind of a dwelling?' the colonel demanded.

The question caught Mustang by surprise.

'Yeah,' he said. 'You're dead right there, colonel.'

'Right about what?'

'It being a dwelling, sir. A ranch house. I did not intrude on the inhabitants, sir. There was smoke coming from the chimney.'

The man's a damn fool, the colonel admitted to himself for the first time. He had tried to deny the fact to himself for one hundred and fifty miles. It had stared him in the face and now, plumb in the middle of a blizzard he had to recognize the fact. They were lost and their only guide was a dumb-head. There was only one way to lose a man of that kind out here and that was to shoot him. The colonel thought: Oh, God, don't tempt me.

He said: 'Smithers, go tell the rancher the army's here. We'll want warm quarters and bait for the horses. Polite, now. You know what these damned civilians are. Rattle your hocks, man. Don't just stand there.'

When the army came into the yard, Lige Copley appeared from the house, wide-eyed. He had never seen so many men in one place in his life. They did not look much like soldiers to him. They were bundled up in any kind of clothing they could find, buffalo robes, blankets, anything to protect them against the cold. When the stout gentleman with the loud voice and the hectoring manner strode into the house and took command, Lige's self-possession nearly deserted him. He did not know what a black boy left in charge of a horse-ranch did when a white man of obvious authority took over his boss's place. He felt responsible and he felt inadequate. This was his first real job and, though tall and physically tough, he was still little more than a child.

He protested and, when he did, the chief soldier (he gathered as he went along that the man was a real live colonel) told him to behave himself or he would find himself under arrest. His men were to be quartered in the barn. He would have turned the horses out, but that was too much for Lige. Fear and respect were one thing, failing in his duty was another. He told the colonel his boss's name and though the colonel claimed he had never heard of it, a couple of the officers with him said they knew it well. For good measure, Lige told them that Colonel James Hickok, none other than the famous Wild Bill, was working for his boss and that he knew how to look out for his employer's interests. This stout colonel may have been impressed by this information. If he was, he did not let it show. He indicated that on the one hand Lige was a liar and, on the other, Colonel James Hickok, esquire, was not worth a heap of beans when it came to the interests of the United States government.

A half-dozen officers moved into the little house, luxuriating in the warmth from the stove. An orderly brought in wood for that same stove and it roared till it was red-hot. The officers demanded food and one of them insisted that Lige break into McAllister's winter supplies for victuals for the men. They would pay for them, they said. In government scrip. Lige had heard about government scrip and knew how long it took for actual cash to be paid over. If ever. He was not a happy boy.

Then, when it came to sleep time, one of the officers objected to having to share sleeping quarters with a black man. On this point, however, Lige would not budge. He knew his rights and stuck to them. The officers agreed to compromise when one of their number (Lige learned he was the major second-in-command) supported Lige's claims. They agreed that he should sleep on the floor.

Lige went to sleep that night, swearing that one day he would get even with the United States army.

There was, however, one incident which somewhat compensated for Lige's humiliation during the evening. This was when Lige asked the major why his regiment had chosen to halt at a ranch when it could have as easily stopped at the town where there would have been much accommodation and certainly more plentiful supplies.

'Town,' said the major, 'what town?'

The colonel sat up abruptly in McAllister's bunk.

'Town?' he cried. 'What town?'

'Black Horse,' said Lige, amazed that they were surprised.

The colonel flung his short legs over the edge of the bunk.

'Do you mean to tell me, boy,' he said, 'that we are in the vicinity of Black Horse?'

Lige gaped at him. 'You mean you didn't know? You must of come plumb past it, mister.'

The colonel was making strangled noises. His face turned a kind of dull purple. Finally he managed to say: 'That goddam scout, that no-good, know-nothing son-of-a-bitch. I'll have his guts for galluses in the morning. My God, he couldn't find the tip of his fool nose.'

Now an idea occurred to Captain Harry Brigg.

'Boy,' he said, 'did you hear any talk of Indians around here?'

'Sure,' said Lige. 'There was a bunch of Indians camped on the north end of the valley. They were on the crick down near the breaks. My boss talked with them.'

'Whose band?' said the colonel, suddenly eager. 'Did you hear?'

'White Bull's.'

The colonel jumped down from the bunk.

'By God,' he cried, 'we've got him. I knew I was headed right. You see where you get if you have faith in yourself, gentlemen? Boy, you will guide us to these Indians at first light.'

Lige looked puzzled and said: 'I don't have no idea where them Indians is at, colonel, and that's a fact.'

'You said they were camped at the north end of this valley,' the colonel accused.

'So they was,' Lige answered. 'But they ain't now.'

'Where'd they go?'

'I don't have no notion, sir.'

The colonel looked fit to be tied.

'So near,' he said, 'and yet so far. But I shall find them. When this McAllister gets home, he will lead us to them. He'll know this country.'

Captain Brigg said: 'He most likely knows these Indians. Well.'

The colonel swung on him. 'You seem to be better informed than I am, captain. What do you know of McAllister and the Cheyenne?'

Brigg said: 'The way I heard it, McAllister was part raised by the Indians.'

'An Indian-lover, huh?' the colonel said, and Lige did not know that he admired the tone the soldier used when he spoke of McAllister. 'We know how to deal with that kind, gentlemen.'

The major said: 'So do we wait here until this McAllister returns, colonel?'

The colonel glared at him and Lige could tell that the two men did not like each other.

'We remain here,' the colonel said, 'until I damn-well say we move.'

The major said: 'I have to remaind you, colonel, that we shall soon over-run our ninety days. With the scrip we have issued for supplies and quarters tonight, we have already overspent our budget considerably.'

The colonel stood staring at the major, clenching and uncleanching his hands in anger.

'I have a better consideration of my duty, sir,' he said, 'than I have of mere economics.'

So that was that. Before he fell asleep on the floor, Lige thought about the Indians. He could not see what the army wanted with a band of Indians who had seemed, according to what his boss had told him, perfectly friendly. He wished that McAllister were there to give this dominating colonel his come-uppance. He had the feeling that, if McAllister walked in here now, all these officers would be out in the snow double-quick.

9.

McAllister did not return to the cave for over two hours and Hickok was beginning to be anxious for him. He knew well enough that McAllister was able to look out for himself, but he also knew that Dom Lawson was a tough and resourceful man.

When McAllister tramped into the firelight and held his frozen hands gratefully to the flames, Hickok said: 'I was beginning to think ole Dom had gotten a bead on you, boy.'

'It's Dom all right, Jim. Him and another fellow, maybe two, are holed up in Greg's cabin.'

'What about Talbot?'

'He's out back with a couple of holes in him.'

Hickok frowned. 'That's something you owe Dom for, I shouldn't wonder.'

'Right.'

They prepared a meal and were thankful to get the hot food into them. They laced their coffee with whisky and McAllister began to thaw out. They did not speak during the meal, but when they were through and McAllister had cleaned the dishes in the snow, they sipped coffee and talked a little, huddled in their buffalo coats close to the fire.

'I aim to hit 'em at dawn,' McAllister said.

Hickok groaned.

'Jesus, how I hate this attack-at-dawn shenanigan,' he said. 'The enemy's always more wide awake than me. I need a good breakfast under my belt and an hour or two to warm up.'

'No call for you to leave your blankets,' said McAllister. 'I can handle these punks.'

'Punks, my ass,' said Hickok. 'And you're being insulting. You need any extra gun you can get against Lawson. I make one stipulation – we're a good distance from the nearest law and nobody ain't going to ask us questions. We settle these boys' hash any which way we can. They're real nasty and they won't see their way to give us an even break, Rem. We see 'em, we shoot and no questions asked.'

McAllister laughed.

'I was thinking along the same lines,' he said. 'I'm set on not letting one of them getting away on Caesar.'

'You bet,' said Hickok. 'Well, let's get some shut-eye. And let's eat before we start out. All right?'

'Keno,' said McAllister. 'Maybe we won't get a chance to eat before the day's out. You got jerky?'

'Never move without a pocketful,' said Hickok.

They broke out their bedrolls and, having built up the fire, they rolled in their blankets and were both asleep within minutes.

10.

He was known officially as Captain William Steiner; but he was not a captain any more. Now he was Bill Steiner and he was an Indian agent. He had an agency of sorts, but the agency did not stand on a reservation. Bill Steiner often wondered why his office had been created, but saw no reason to raise any great objection about its conditions. He had come out of the army tired of campaigning and never getting promotion and tired of being broke on army pay. He was still broke.

His main trouble was that he was honest. He had been an honest soldier and now he was an honest Indian agent. Honest soldiers were not so rare, but around that time honest Indian agents were pretty hard to find.

As to his duties – they never seemed too clear to him, but he assumed that he was there to look after the interests of the Indians, peaceful Indians that is, and to see that they behaved themselves. How he was supposed to make them behave themselves if they had no wish to, he had no idea, except that he could call on the army.

His agency consisted of a storehouse and a fairly roomy cabin some twelve miles south-west of the fort. At the fort, Major Robert Whitehouse commanded. Whitehouse and Steiner had served together in the Army of the West on a number of campaigns and their antipathy was mutual. Neither knew why, except that they were opposites. Whitehouse was pompous and a stickler, Steiner was an easy-going fellow, not short on courage or conscience, but one to live and let live. Steiner never felt about Indians in the way Whitehouse did. Steiner considered that the Indian had some arguments in his favour. Whitehouse did not. It was as simple as that.

At his little agency, Steiner was supported by not one

single Indian policeman, but only by a clerk whose mother had been a Sioux of the Oglalla people. He could read and write and he spoke both Sioux and Cheyenne. When they had some free time the clerk, Sammy Samson, was teaching the agent Sioux. Snowed in now they had plenty of time for their studies.

Tonight, with the stove red-hot and the coffee pot boiling, Bill Steiner was uneasy. His mind would not concentrate on the lesson Sammy was giving him. He looked across at the man and studied the flat Sioux face, the skin so light for an Indian. He did not get the lightness from his American father. Many Sioux were as pale. His eyes were wholly Indian and often Stenier could not read him. But the halfbreed was a good man, steady, intelligent and holding his own with dignity in an increasingly white world.

Steiner stood up abruptly and walked to the window. He could hear the wind howling outside, the crack of a tree snapping off in the icy blast. The night was pitch-black. The snow had stopped falling and lay level with the window sill.

Sammy said: 'What's fretting you, boss?'

'Everything's fretting me, Sammy. Goddam everything.'

If Sammy felt any sympathy his face showed nothing.

He said: 'Nothing can happen in this weather, captain.'

The agent turned from the window and said: 'Washita happened in this weather. Does history repeat itself? Could that happen again here?'

Sammy did not know what to say to that. That kind of thing could always happen to his mother's people. Such things would happen until the troubles between the Indians and the whites came to an end. And he knew how it must end. A patch of brown bodies would be lying in the snow or in the dust and the blue-coated soldiers would stand around grinning for the photographer. The newspaper headlines would call the killing a battle. If the reverse had been true and the bodies on the ground had been soldiers, that would be called a massacre.

Without believing what he said, he told the agent: 'Nobody would dare, captain.'

Steiner said: 'Did you ever see Colonel Brevington?'

Suddenly, Sammy was alive. His eyes showed his feelings abruptly with a sudden ferocity that startled the agent.

'Sure,' he said. 'I saw him.'

Stenier knew there was a story here. When two men were alone for a long period as they would be, they talked. It was inevitable.

Steiner walked back across the room and poured them both a cup of coffee. Sammy remembered when he had first seen the man ten years before. Steiner had been leading a patrol against the Cheyenne down in southern Kansas. He had to contact the Indians and, if possible, talk with them. Sammy had gone along as an interpreter. It was then that Sammy realized that he was accompanying a man who was just not another army officer. This man had some understanding and some imagination. Maybe too much of both for his own good.

They had got themselves into a tight spot. It had been a winter campaign. The weather had been almost as bad as this. Surprisingly, they had found some Indians: a band of Cheyenne under the chief Many Horses. And old Many Horses at that time was in his prime and not in any kind of mood to touch a humble forelock to an army man no matter how many guns he commanded.

Steiner had realized that if he started the shooting match, a blood-bath would follow. There were women and children there. So he and Many Horses had talked. And they did so through Sammy. Never in his life had he been more careful how he translated two men's words for them. He knew there were subtle nuances in the talk and he did his level best to keep them when he put them into a very alien language.

The upshot of it had been that Many Horses had promised that he would not raid any more that winter. He and his people had sufficient food till spring. He would stay still and he promised that his young men would do the same.

Then Sammy had told Steiner: 'This Indian is a fighting man, captain, and he would fight quick enough if he had to. But he has given his word and I never heard that he broke it. Was I you, I'd shake his hand and believe him.'

And that was what Steiner had done. Sammy heard later

that he had lost his chance of promotion by so doing.

A simple friendship had grown up between the army captain and the halfbreed. They understood each other so far as two men with such disparate backgrounds could. They had gone out on other missions together in later years. When Steiner had left the army and taken the job of agent (fixed, it was said, by a cousin in Washington), he had asked Sammy to join him.

Now when Sammy looked at his superior he saw a man who was physically not half the man he had been. He had grown stout. Soon, he would be fat. His jowls had thickened and his hair thinned. But his eyes still retained their amused humanity.

Sammy thought: He is a good man born with bad luck. And the thought made him sad, for he had a great respect for Steiner.

He thought of Sand Creek and a shudder went through him. All America had shuddered or been exhilarated by the killing of men, women and children in the Cheyenne-Arapaho camp. The Colorado Volunteers under the infamous Colonel Chivington had done their work thoroughly. Young white boys, under the orders and example of their elders and superiors, had become berserk killers. Christian opinion had been horrified. There were courts-martial. Chivington had been a famous lay-preacher.

Just as Colonel Brevington was.

'What happened, Sammy?'

The captain's question brought Sammy back into the present.

'You'd maybe not think the story worth hearing, boss.'

'Try me.'

'There's not much to it.'

'Now you're making me real curious.'

Sammy laughed. 'Just I was in this church. Not being white, I sat at the back. I listened to this preacher. It was hell-fire and brimstone stuff and he talk about the Indian being the Amalakite. He even talked about the only good Indian being a dead one.'

Steiner said: 'Brevington?'

'Yes. But that wasn't all. He spotted me. And he had me thrown out of there, shouting about how he wasn't going to pray in the same church as an Indian. He could see from my face that I was a Sioux, he said. Sure, there was one or two who protested that we were in the house of the Lord. But that didn't wash with Brevington. So I was thrown out.'

'Enough to turn a man heathen,' Steiner said.

Sammy smiled. 'It did that to young George Bent, but not to me.'

George Bent had been the halfbreed son of one of the great Bent brothers who had been in the Indian camp during the Sand Creek massacre. After that he had reverted to Indian in spite of his education and had run wild against the whites.

'So now,' Steiner said, 'that preacher's a colonel and he's commanding two hundred and fifty men. He's hunting Indians and he don't know one Indian from another. What's more, he don't care. Every Indian in sight is a hostile.'

Sammy said: 'You seem to know this man.'

'I know him all right.'

'What about the major at the fort?'

Steiner gave a short, braking laugh.

'The major is not going to push his nose out of the fort in this weather. I don't think I would either in his boots. He's built the fort and the Sioux have watched him put every log on top of another.'

Sammy said: 'I can't be sure, of course, but I'd say there wasn't a war-party within a hundred miles of here.'

The agent looked at his clerk with interest: Sammy did not make claims like that for nothing. 'You sure of that?'

'I can't be one hundred per cent sure, captain. But that's my feeling.'

'Well, your feelings have been right enough in the past.'

Suddenly his attention was taken by one of the dogs asleep near the stove. The wolflike animal sat up abruptly, looking towards the door, ears forward. As it began to growl, its mate also started up. They bared their teeth. Sammy rose quickly and lifted his rifle down from its hooks on the wall.

As something slammed against the door, both dogs launched themselves forward, barking and snarling ferociously. Through it the two men thought they heard a half-human voice wailing in tune with the wind outside.

Sammy beat back the dogs with the butt of his rifle and put his mouth close to the door. He shouted something in Sioux and there came a reply. Over his shoulder, he told Steiner: 'It's a Sioux. Do I open?'

'Sure you open.'

Just the same, the Indian agent reached for his own rifle. He had been too long on the frontier to be caught easily with his pants down. He stood well back from the door while Sammy lifted the bar on it and stepped back, taking the door sideways with him.

A dark, pinched face seemed to lurch and swing out of the dark night at them. The figure of a man emerged from the night, brows frosted. He was alone, and as he stepped into the heat of the cabin he seemed to have his very breath taken away by the warmth. Sammy hastily shut the door and propped his rifle against the wall. He put an arm around the frozen Indian and half-carried him to a chair.

Steiner simply looked at the man and said: 'My God!'

His exclamation expressed his astonishment that a man so flimsily clothed could have survived the weather outside. He poured hot coffee and dropped a little whisky into it. The Indian's hands were too frozen to hold the cup. Sammy held it for him and let him sip at the hot liquid.

Now his face was all pinched up with the cold, his eyes showing them that the cold had been and was still a physical agony to him. He wore nothing more than a hunting shirt, breech-clout, leggings and tattered moccasins. He had draped a threadbare blanket over his head and shoulders. The only weapon he carried was a knife in a beaded scabbard at his side.

As the man crouched in the chair, watching the hot stove and sipping at the coffee, he said nothing. Sammy talked to him softly in his own language.

An hour later, the man spoke. It seemed to take a great effort to get the words from his constricted throat. Sammy reckoned he was pretty ill besides being badly frozen. The man wanted almost to hug the stove, but Sammy prevented him from getting too close to it. After an hour, the pinched look in his dark face had almost gone. His eyes came alive. Now he started to talk. Every now and then, Sammy interpreted for Steiner and slowly they shared his story.

He came from the camp of White Bull, he said.

Steiner queried that at once. He had great sympathy for the Indians in general but that did not mean they could easily pull the wool over his eyes. If he came from White Bull's camp, how was it that he was so badly equipped? Steiner had been in White Bull's camp and, while the Indians there had not been exactly rich, they looked as if they were well enough supplied.

The Indian did not like that question much when Sammy put it to him.

'And while you're asking him that,' Steiner said, 'ask him what a Sioux is doing in a Cheyenne camp?'

'That's possible, captain,' Sammy said. 'We both know that. The Sioux and Cheyenne are allies.'

'When did you last see a Sioux in a small band of Cheyenne's winter camp?'

'I would not call him a liar for saying it,' Sammy persisted. 'He may be in the same society as some of the Cheyenne. The societies go across tribal lines.'

But that did not satisfy Steiner.

He said: 'Sammy, ask him if there is food in White Bull's camp?'

Sammy put the question. The man answered very shortly.

'Captain, he says there is very little food in the camp. Soon the children will be crying because there will be no food left.'

Steiner paced up and down the floor a few times.

'It don't wash, Sammy. When we were in that camp, there were supplies aplenty.' Their eyes met. Sammy knew the answer to that and he was not saying. 'We both know that a bunch of refugees from the fighting has taken shelter in that camp. And old White Bull feels obliged to feed them. Or maybe they threatened him and took what they wanted. Ask this fellow how many warriors have run from the soldiers and taken shelter in White Bull's camp.'

Sammy looked a little doubtful and Steiner had to say:

'Go ahead, ask it,' before he once more spoke to the Indian.

The man look worried and cast a half-scared look at Steiner.

Sammy said: 'He said there has been no fight with the soldiers. He and a few friends were caught by the snow at the end of a hunt and they stumbled by accident on White Bull's camp.'

Steiner thought about that for a while and then said: 'I'll accept all of that except the crap about being on a hunt. The only hunt this s.o.b. has been on is after whitemen.' He glared at Sammy, as if inviting him to challenge that statement; but Sammy had been suspended mentally between the Indians and the whites for too long to fall for that kind of thing. He knew that Steiner knew what was in his mind – this very Indian had possibly been committing savage atrocities not so many days before . . . and they could not blame him. The whites had done it to his people, were still doing it. You did not expect a savage to behave like a Christian. Neither did you expect a Christian to behave like a savage.

They both knew the problem would not be solved while the Indian lived. When the Indian had disappeared along with the antelope and the buffalo, when the whiteman could no longer be reminded that he had wiped out a whole breed of man . . .

At that moment Steiner wished that he had abandoned the West. He should have shucked the West along with his uniform, gone back East where it was possible to lead a civilized life with books and pretty women.

Now the Sioux was talking. It was as though the warmth of the cabin had at last succeeded in loosening his tongue. He spoke to Sammy, but his eyes were on Steiner. It was the agent whom he had to convince. Now he was pleading for his people, no longer playing the proud warrior. He desperately wanted help for his people . . . in this case the band of Cheyenne somewhere to the south. Sammy began translating, putting the Indian's eloquent Lakotah into eloquent English until finally Steiner's nerve seemed to crack under the weight of it all and he cried: 'All right, all right,

Sammy. For Christ's sake, you don't have to labour the point, man. We'll get help to them somehow.'

'Wouldn't it be better if they could come here, boss?' Sammy asked. 'They're scared. They know that the soldiers at the fort don't want them in the vicinity. They know Brevington and his merry men are searching the country for any Indians they can find. If they were here under the American flag, they'd feel safe.'

'No,' said Steiner very definitely. 'Not here. We'll go to them, Sammy. We have to.'

'It'll take some doing,' said Sammy. 'Maybe it's not even possible. The weather's getting worse by the day.'

'We have to try. There's women and children there. We'll pack a sled with supplies. We'll take them a US flag they can sit under. Nobody would touch them with the Stars and Stripes over them.' He hesitated and said: 'Just the same, I don't feel too damned happy about giving an amnesty to a bunch of renegade Sioux.'

Sammy kept his mouth shut. He had got what he wanted – supplies to the People.

'When do we start?' he asked.

'First light,' said Steiner. 'Give this fellow some blankets and let him bed down here. Is he strong enough to guide us back?'

Sammy spoke to the Sioux. The man grunted and Sammy said: 'He'll do it.'

11.

When a man like Hickok demanded breakfast before he went out to do a job, he got what he wanted. Bacon and beans went into the pan an hour before daylight. Shortly after, it was washed down by scalding hot coffee. With his mouth full, McAllister explained what he intended.

His main aim was to get his precious stallion back.

Meting justice out to the thieves was a bonus which chance might offer them. He was going ahead and would be in position by daylight to lift his own horse. What he wanted Hickok to do was bring these two horses to the near-end of the break in which the outlaws' horses were penned. He would find sufficient shelter for them there where they could be hidden from Lawson and the others if they came for their own horses. After Hickok had tied the horses, he could work his way down the break and be in position by first light to cover McAllister when he made a break for it on Caesar's back.

'Ain't you forgetting one thing, Rem?' Hickok asked.

'What's that?'

'For one, Lawson can shoot the eye out of gnat.'

'I'm not forgetting it, Jim. Can you think of any other way of making sure Dom don't ride off on my horse. If he does that, neither of us could risk a shot at him for fear of hitting the stud.'

'Maybe Dom'll have the same qualm,' said Hickok dryly. 'Just remember, I don't see so good with my eyes this way.'

'Just be damn sure you don't shoot me,' McAllister said. A thought hit him and he cursed himself for not thinking of it before. 'Jim, is the snow playing hell with your eyes?'

Calmly, Hickok said: 'Let's say it don't help.'

They saddled the horses together. McAllister left his rifle in the saddleboot. If he was up on Caesar bareback, he did not want to be encumbered by a rifle. They killed the fire. Hickok said: 'Time's getting on. I'll come with you now so you can ride and save a little time.'

It seemed like a good idea. McAllister said: 'All right, let's go.' Outside the snow had stopped falling and the surface of the snow on the ground was hardened by the extreme cold of the night. They rode their horses a good way before the surface broke suddenly beneath the animals' hard hooves. Cursing a little, they dismounted to get their horses out of the soft snow. They sank deep themselves, fought their horses out on to a firmer footing and then promptly fell into a deep drift. Now, McAllister took the lead on foot and broke trail. It was getting dangerously near daylight by the time they led the horses down into the break. At this far end from the house, they found a fairly sheltered spot where some dwarf conifers grew and where snow-laden boulders lay strewn. They tied the horses and Hickok urged McAllister to hurry ahead or he would be caught in the open by daylight.

McAllister at once started down the break and pretty soon came to the loose horses. He found that he could not climb out of the break and avoid them, though he wanted to, for if he disturbed them they could alarm the men in the cabin. He stopped as they stirred uneasily at his approach, and spoke to them in a low and, he hoped, reassuring voice. The sorrel looked as if he did not like mankind in general and McAllister in particular. He kicked up his heels and whickered loudly and McAllister mentally slew him a few times. He hurried over the brush barricade, which was now plastered with snow, and got among some pines to the left of the mouth of the break. From here he could clearly see two sides of the cabin and the shed. Smoke trickled from the stone chimney. He thought he heard a man's voice, muffled, but could not be sure. He began edging his way through the pines, watching the cabin carefully the whole time. Pretty soon, he had the shed between himself and the cabin. Getting to his feet he began to tread his laborious way through the snow to the rear of the shed.

As he approached it, he was glad to see that it was not in the best of repair. It was constructed crudely of thick, upright planks of wood, green and warped. He supposed it provided some kind of shelter for the horse inside, but he reckoned it would still be pretty draughty. He put his eye to a wide crack between planks and saw at once that Caesar was aware of his presence. The horse was standing within a few feet of him, head up and ears forward.

McAllister drew his gun and used it as a lever to prise the gap wider. As he did so, the stallion rumbled his greeting. If they had not heard the sound in the cabin, they must have been deaf.

In spite of the cold, he started to sweat. He swore a little. The planks might be green and warped, but they seemed immovable. He put the gun away, gripped the edge of a plank with both hands and bore his weight back from it. Nails screamed as they began to loosen. He brought the flat of one foot up against the wall of the shed to increase his leverage. With an ear-splitting crack, the plank came free in his hands and he fell back headlong into the snow.

As he hit the snow, so he heard the crack of a rifle.

As he staggered to his feet, he thought he heard a muffled shout or two from the cabin.

The rifle cracked out again and he heard Hickok bellow: 'This is Hickok, Lawson. You put your fool head outside of there and I'll blow the goddam thing off. Hear?'

There was a short burst of firing. McAllister got hold of a second plank and started to give it the treatment he had given the first. This one came away more willingly. He stooped quickly and found himself inside the shed. At once he felt the warmth which had accumulated there from the horse. Caesar now showed his excitement at the appearance of McAllister. He knew that his arrival meant action and that was what his young blood wanted more than anything.

McAllister slapped him a couple of times on the neck, then went to the door and tried to open it a crack. The weight of the snow outside prevented him from moving it more than an inch or so. This enabled him to see the full side of the cabin and the front at an acute angle. The door of the cabin was open slightly and the black line of a rifle barrel showed there.

McAllister ducked back just in time as a bullet splintered the edge of the door and thudded into the far wall of the shed. This at once worried the man who was scared that his horse might be hit.

He returned to the door down on one knee, lined up his Remington with the dark opening of the cabin and fired two shots. That done, he put his gun away and backed up.

Now he took a hasty look around the shed.

Old Greg's tools were hung on nails on the walls and in one corner. There was a heavy sledge-hammer among them. He heaved a pile of hay away from the rear wall and, now having room to move, he attacked the planks with the sledge-hammer. In no time at all he had removed a number of them.

Then he smashed the support rail and there was an opening wide enough for a horse to pass through.

There was a bridle hanging from a nail and a saddle in hessian sacking in a corner. He untied Caesar and moved him away from the door. The animal stood obediently while McAllister saddled him.

Holding the horse's lines, he stepped out into the snow again and looked toward the mouth of the break. Hickok fired a shot and McAllister was able to locate him at once. Now McAllister waved an arm to attract Hickok's attention. Hickok shouted: 'Go ahead.' Then he started firing again, no doubt placing his shots through the oiled-paper of the window on his side of the cabin. McAllister pulled the horse out into the open and vaulted into the saddle.

Now came the part he did not like. He intended to make a dash for the trees. Three or four jumps by Caesar and he would be in sight of the men in the cabin. A horse in deep snow is not the fastest thing in the world. Lawson's bullets would be as fast as ever.

Caesar was dancing with eagerness.

McAllister kicked the stud in the belly and yelled to it. The canelo leapt forward and hit running. He went along the trail packed by McAllister's approach to the shed. As though from a long way off, McAllister heard the sound of a gun in the cabin. If any shots came near him, he was not aware of them. The wind cut cold across his face from the stud's speed. It seemed that almost instantly they were among the trees and the horse was weaving his path, this way and that, through them.

They went about one hundred yards into timber before McAllister swung the stud to the left and headed back towards the break. When he was near enough for his voice to carry to Hickok, he reined in and shouted. Hickok's bellow came back. McAllister wanted Wild Bill to pull back, but the gunfighter refused. McAllister slipped from the saddle and tied the stud. It was not content, for it still wanted to run.

McAllister was thinking about old Greg Talbot, killed and tossed carelessly into the snow. He stood close to the bole of a pine and wondered what Dom Lawson would do now.

That the man could not excape from the cabin without his horses, McAllister was almost certain, though there was no telling what a mad dog like that one would do. McAllister and Hickok were between the cabin and the outlaws' horses.

A small voice inside McAllister's head told him: You have your horse. Get out while the going's good.

But he know that he would not. Talbot had died because of that same horse.

Hickok's rifle was silent. The men in the cabin had ceased firing. The silence extended itself. Finally, McAllister became uneasy. That silence could mean any number of things. Maybe Lawson was low on ammunition. Maybe the men had sneaked from the cabin on the blind side. Something cold and wet touched his cheek. The snow had started to fall again.

He showed his hat around the tree, but nothing happened.

The cold was beginning to get to McAllister and he started to shiver. Looking toward Hickok's position, he saw that the gunfighter was on his feet, rifle in hands and his eyes on the cabin.

McAllister stepped out from behind his tree. Nothing happened. He glanced at Hickok and saw that he had seen him. Hickok started working his way through the brush barrier. Snow fell from it like a curtain. He saw Hickok flounder in the snow to his waist and then come on again. McAllister shucked his right-hand glove so that he could handle his gun more easily. He circled to the left and Hickok took the other side of the house. They both watched the solitary window, ready to shoot anybody who appeared at it.

Suddenly, Hickok shouted and pointed. McAllister knew that he had spotted a man out in the main break. McAllister began a clumsy slow run through the thick snow. Once, he floundered into a deep drift in a small gully. By the time he had climbed out of it, Hickok had gone from sight around the far side of the cabin. McAllister hit firmer footing and went forward at a fair pace.

Greg Talbot had shored up the terrace-like rise of ground to the front of the cabin with rocks so that the whole of the ground on which the cabin stood looked as if it were man-made. He had edged this with a stone wall. The whole was now covered with snow, but the wall was still evident. As McAllister rounded the corner of the house, a man's head and shoulders appeared on the far side of this. He snapped a shot off. Glancing right, McAllister saw Hickok standing knee-deep in snow with a pistol in each hand. Wild Bill was the only man McAllister had ever known to shoot this way with two weapons.

As the man fired, so Hickok fired twice, one shot from each weapon.

The man let out a short hoarse cry and fell back out of sight.

Hickok, pistols smoking, said coldly: 'Where's the other son-of-a-bitch? Can you see him?' McAllister could see nothing moving.

Nothing seemed to move on the white landscape. He darted his gaze everywhere, uncomfortably aware that a shot might come at any second and a bullet find its mark in his body.

The thought hit him that there might be a man behind them in the cabin, lining his gun up for a shot. Turning, he jumped for the open doorway, shouting for Hickok to watch his back.

Nothing moved inside the cabin, except for the lifting of a weak hand from Talbot's bunk. The grey face of Dufay showed over the side of the bunk.

'I'm bleeding to death,' he said.

McAllister turned and walked outside. Together he and Hickok walked to the low wall, climbed over and inspected the man lying in the snow on the far side. This was Honniger. They both knew him. Hickok had shot him through head and heart. Exactly the way Greg Talbot had died. McAllister wondered if that had been intentional. He knew that Wild Bill was superstitious.

Hickok said briefly: 'If ever a man needed killing . . . '

McAllister looked around.

'Dom Lawson is somewheres out there,' he said.

Hickok nodded. 'We'd best clear out of here before he plants a bullet in one of our backs.'

Now McAllister thought of Caesar and realized that the man might have headed for the stud. The way Lawson felt about horses, he would be tempted to risk his neck for the animal. McAllister started running, slipping and stumbling in the snow. When he reached Caesar, he was pretty breathless, but at least he had worked up a little sweat and no longer shook with cold. The animal was safe and sound and as pleased as ever to see McAllister again.

The two men brought all the horses in near to the house and gave them a feed of Talbot's hay. They debated what to do about the wounded man.

Hickok said: 'Knowing this son-of-a-bitch, I've a mind to leave him to rot.'

'But we won't,' McAllister said.

'I guess not, goddammit.'

They cut poles and constructed a travois. McAllister was in a pretty evil temper, because hauling this man through the snow would slow them up and he wanted to reach home. Neither thought the travois was practicable in snow, nor was it. So they wasted more time making a litter. It was noon before they were ready to move. By this time, it was McAllister who expressed the idea of abandoning the wounded man. To bely his words, he put a fresh dressing on the wound and declared with some show of regret that he thought the fellow would live. They had quite a chore getting the heavy man plus a buffalo coat into the litter, but after a good deal of heaving and shoving they made it. Once in the litter, the man complained that he was cold. They did not pay too much attention to him. They were also cold.

Hickok said when they were mounted: 'We'd best keep our eyes skinned, Rem. That bastard Lawson may be laying for us.'

Dufay heard that. He said: 'Laying for you. You two ain't going to live the goddam day out.'

'Aw, hell,' Hickok said, 'my vote says we dump him in the snow and leave him.'

But with profound regret, they did not. Slowly, they made their way out of the breaks and headed along Black Horse Valley.

12.

If Captain William Steiner never did anything else in his life which was, in his poor opinion of himself, worth remembering, he would never forget that trip through the snow with the Sioux Indian and Sammy Samson. He was never quite sure why he did it, except that maybe he wanted to do something worthwhile before he died. He knew that back in the regiment his fellow-officers would have laughed at him for it or been angered by it. Who the hell cared a cent's worth about a passle of goddam Indian?

There were most likely two ideas in the ex-army officer's mind. One, that he was an Indian agent and the Indians were his responsibility; two (and this he shied from admitting to himself) he could not sit still while women and children died in the terrible winter through cold and starvation. He had seen it happen before.

The going was bad and, until he reached the point of no return, the idea of turning back occurred to him frequently. He never gave way to it because his two companions obviously had no thought in their heads but to reach White Bull's band and save it.

There had been some debate between Steiner and Sammy about whether they should attempt to take horses, but they decided against it. They loaded the single sled with all it would take in the way of supplies and blankets and left the agency in the sole care of an old halfbreed trapper and his Indian wife. The three men harnessed themselves to that sled like beasts and walked, or so Steiner thought, forever. Their great asset was that not only did the Sioux have a fair idea of which way to go, but also Sammy Samson possessed an almost perfect memory for country through which he had once passed. As he said, country looked very different under snow from ordinary times, but, just the same, he guided them unerringly. This in itself must have saved them miles and hours of needless travel. As it was, after five hours of pulling on the heavily laden sled, Steiner, softened by a year or more of soft living, too much food and drink and not enough hours in the saddle, found progress a torture.

But he denied himself the relief of surrender, for he had made up his mind that, if his two companions could make it, he could also. Maybe, he hold himself as he slogged through the snow, his luck had turned. A day out from the agency, they came quite by accident on a solitary mule-deer nibbling the twigs of a tree and Sammy dropped it with one shot. They butchered it at once, gorged on deermeat and packed what was left on to the complaining sled.

They saw the fires of the camp on the evening of the second day.

It was a cluster of buffalo-hide tents in a shallow dell on the edge of a frozen creek. Later, when he checked it on a map, Steiner found that it was called Dead Indian Creek.

The first thing the agent noticed about it was its utter defencelessness. It could be attacked across open land on the creek side. It could be attacked from a ridge on the west, covered with pines. To the south, running down the slope and clustered along the edge of the creek were birches and willows and here was what was left of the horse-herd. There were no guards on the animals. In this weather they were not going anywhere, except to maybe drift before the wind. Certainly nobody was going to come to steal them.

The night, he remembered later, was a particularly beautiful one. The sky had cleared itself of cloud and the moon rode serenely amid an ocean of stars, bright and cold in a dark half-sphere. The temperature had dropped. When a man spat, the spittle crackled in the air.

Not only the horses were unguarded. The whole encampment was without a sentinel. He did not know if this demonstrated trust or despair. The Sioux with them, now a familiar, addressed as Hawk and admitting to a little English, shouted out that he was here with food. That brought them from the tipis, huddled against the cold, faces drawn, tight lips sucking reluctantly on the icy air. They stood and gazed in wonder at the treasures that had been brought.

Steiner said to Sammy: 'Just forget your Sioux part, Sam. I have to know if the Sioux here have been in a fight with the soldiers. It's important. It'll make all the difference to how I play this.'

Sammy nodded. Whether that meant he would do so or merely that he understood, Steiner could not tell. He caught Sammy by the sleeve – 'I want to know if any of them are wounded.'

'All right, captain,' Sammy said. 'We both know they've been fighting and we know some of them will be wounded.'

'I have to be sure.'

White Bull appeared in front of him. They did not know each other well, but they had met a couple of times. In their alien but close worlds, both knew to a nicety the other's reputation. The Cheyenne knew Steiner for a just man, a former soldier who had fought the Cheyenne. Steiner put White Bull down as a wise old bird who was trying to survive in an almost impossible world. Among Indians he was known as a straight man who kept his word. Whether his word was good with a whiteman was another matter. Steiner might sympathize with the Indians in their terrible predicament, but he was nobody's fool.

They shook hands and Sammy gave the Indian Steiner's greeting. White Bull returned the greeting politely and with dignity. His manner was a mixture of relief and anxiety. Steiner guessed that his relief at the supplies reaching him was profound. At the same time, he must be acutely nervous because of the presence of the Sioux warriors in his camp. He invited Steiner into the warmth of his tent. Steiner asked that the supplies be put in a safe place. They were limited and they would have to be rationed out carefully. That, White Bull suggested, should be the responsibility of the Kit Fox chief. That was the society then doing police duty for the band. There were three Kit Foxes in his band and they were highly responsible men. Steiner agreed.

Inside the tent, the agent was almost suffocated by the heat, the smell of human bodies, food and other domestic smells that clung to an Indian home. At the same time, it was vastly reassuring to know that such warmth and primitive comfort still existed. With enormous relief, he shucked his heavy buffalo coat and relaxed on a hide rug, leaning against a back-rest. He sighed his contentment and old White Bull smiled. Through Sammy he said that Steiner had come a long way and that he was a good man. They were not starving, but they had been on short rations for some days. If he had not come, they would all have suffered greatly. Game, it seemed, had departed before the snow. Sammy gave the deer meat to the chief's women and they had it into the pot over the fire in no time at all. Steiner's stomach juices went wild at the smell of the stewing venison.

After the leisurely exchanges of polite Indian society, but in a shorter time than was usual, they got down to cases. The women chattered softly among themselves. One of them, White Bull's daughter probably, was a remarkably fine-looking girl, dark for a Cheyenne and with delicate features. She was very shy with Steiner in the tent. Three or four little children, dark-eyed and full of wonder, concentrated their gazes hard on the whiteman. Two young men watched the agent with expressionless faces. Steiner asked the chief if he and his family would care for a little whisky. The chief said that he had no objection to spirits in moderation. Everybody there, except the children, helped Steiner empty his small flask and that seemed to break the ice a little. Even the young men were able to unfreeze their faces a little. Steiner made White Bull a present of some tobacco. The old man's smile broadened. Later, perhaps, they would smoke the pipe together. Steiner nodded and smiled.

Suddenly, they were launched into serious talk. Steiner would speak, Sammy would translate and the old man would sit and think calmly before making his reply. After a while, he asked Steiner if he had any objection to two of the elders joining them. Steiner had no objection. They exchanged pleasantries while a youngster fetched the men.

One was a tall, handsome man with a grave, triangular face; an experienced man, but scarcely old enough to be called an elder. He looked intelligent, quick and, at first, slightly resentful of the whiteman. His name was Walks-a-Long-Time. The other was a man older than the chief, bent of back and white-haired. He seemed to be half-asleep when he entered and to drop off to sleep completely when he settled himself down. He was called Old Horse.

White Bull appeared not to refer to either of them in the talk that followed. For the most part, they listened (or at least Walks did), but neither spoke. It became clear to Steiner that White Bull was convinced that the army did not intend to protect his band. He had brought his people here to get well clear of the fighting so that the soldiers would know beyond all doubt that they had not taken part in attacks on the soldiers or anybody else.

'I have brought with me an American flag,' Steiner said. 'No soldier would fire on his own flag. You know that it is sacred to us.'

The chief nodded. Yes, he knew that. At dawn, they would put up the flag. That would make them all feel better. Already he felt better.

Now what he wanted was for the chief at the fort to allow him and his people to move near the fort as soon as it was possible so that they would be safe. Once there, the soldiers would know for sure that White Bull was not fighting against the soldiers. Then there could be no doubt in their minds.

Steiner spread his hands. It was to be greatly regretted, but this would not be possible. He would speak yet again to the soldier chief at the fort, but it would do little good. He would not permit the Indians to come nearer than they were now. He was sorry, but there was nothing he could do about it.

The old man did not accept that. He thought that everything in sight was negotiable. Steiner explained again and again that his authority was limited. Ah, said the chief, but Steiner was a well-known and influential man . . . He persisted until Steiner's patience began to be stretched beyond its endurance. He was tired to the bone and the heat of the tent was getting to him. By the time the food was ready to eat, he was almost asleep and was fighting yawns.

'Jesus Christ,' he said to Sammy close at his side, 'I've brought the old devil food, he can have the Stars and Stripes waving over his camp – what the hell more can I do?'

'Nothing,' said Sammy, 'but he has to keep on trying. He's thinking of the lives of everybody in this camp.'

'Do you think I don't know it?' Suddenly, he shot at Sammy: 'Ask him how many Sioux came in with Hawk.'

He saw Sammy's look of alarm. The interpreter hesitated.

Steiner said: 'Go ahead, ask him.'

'The time's not right, captain.'

'I'll decide that.'

'There's only two of us.'

'White Bull wouldn't harm us, for God's sake. He needs us.'

'He's old and sensible. His fighting men are young and not so sensible. Let's take it easy and get to it slowly.'

'You ask him like I said, Sam. And you ask him that exactly.'

Sammy put a question to the chief. Whether he asked the right question, Steiner had no way of knowing. When he saw the looks on the other Indians' faces, he guessed Sammy had been honest. They all looked startled, then worried. Walks looked dangerous. Steiner guessed he *was* dangerous. Steiner wondered if he had been fighting the soldiers lately.

White Bull thought about his answer very carefully.

His reply was definite and short.

Sammy translated: 'He says that he has not been out against the soldiers. That is true, I think, as far as it goes.'

'And it don't go far enough,' said Steiner. 'Put the question to him again, Sam. Bluntly. Don't dress it up. I have to know. We're through with all the polite nonsense. Get it into his head that I'm trying to look after his interests.'

'And he's trying to look after the interests of his band, boss.'

Steiner was impatient. 'Do you think I don't know that? Sometimes you talk as if I have a block of wood on my shoulders. I'm trying to save the old fool in spite of himself. Just try and pull along with me, will you Sam, for God's sake?'

'Captain, where would be the harm in them coming close to the agency? That would satisfy the old man.'

'Because it'd bring them close to the fort. Whitehouse is so goddam jumpy, anything could happen. White Bull is out of sight here. The weather's bad. He could do worse than stay right where he's at.'

Sammy nodded reluctantly. 'I suppose you're right.' He turned and talked for a long time with the chief. It sounded to Steiner as if he was really trying. He hoped so.

Finally, White Bull went into one of his long periods of thought and Steiner started to nod off. Sammy nudged him and his head jerked up. For a moment, Steiner did not know where he was. Then he became aware that the chief was talking in his own language. Walks-a-Long-Time woke Old Horse. The old man started to nod and suck his gums noisily. White Bull talked for some time. When he was through Walks had his turn. Then Old Horse spoke in a weak, high-pitched voice which gradually faded away until he appeared to be asleep once more. White Bull spoke at length to Sammy. Steiner had no idea how Sammy could remember all that stuff. The interpreter gave it to Steiner in brief.

'White Bull says that they are agreed. They will stay here. He says yes, he has some young men in camp who have been fighting the soldiers. But he cannot surrender them to you.'

Now Steiner's patience nearly broke.

'I'm not asking him to.'

'I told him that,' Sammy said. 'They are very happy about the American flag. They believe you are right and that the soldiers will not fire on the flag or anybody under its protection. They say this, but I don't think they believe it. They're afraid.'

Steiner said: 'I can't do any more.'

'They know that. They're grateful. They're surprised you have done so much.' Sammy added: 'Captain, let's hit the sack. I'm bushed.'

'Sure.'

Sammy spoke to the chief and then told Steiner that the chief wanted him to sleep there in the tipi. He could not offer the agent a tent for himself. The people were over-crowding what tents they had. Steiner said that he would be happy to sleep anywhere.

By now, the meat was cooked. They all ate, the Indians with evident satisfaction. Steiner was asleep almost before he was through eating. He was dimly aware that they were waking Old Horse and that the two elders were leaving the tipi. Then Steiner was deep in sleep.

13.

Halfway along Black Horse Valley, McAllister reined in his horse.

'Look'ee here,' he said. 'The army.'

Hickok squinted his poor eyes and said: 'I can't see a damn thing but snow.'

McAllister said: 'A whole goddam regiment of cavalry.' Then he said several impolite words and added: 'And they have Lige along with 'em. I'll have his balls for bed-knobs leaving the horses.'

Hickok said: 'If it's the army, maybe he didn't have too much choice.'

McAllister sat his saddle and watched the army's slow and laborious approach. The men were leading their horses. A couple of officers in the van were still mounted. One of them was a stout gentleman with eye-glasses and a large buffalo coat. McAllister described him to Hickok and the gunfighter said: 'That has to be Arnie Brevington. Now we're in for an earful of wind. He'll bore the ass off you, that one. He has a whole goddam spiel about manifest destiny and the contamination of the savage Indian.'

'One of those, huh?'

As soon as they were near, Lige hurried forward and started to say: 'Boss, I didn't have no choice. These here soldier-boys, they – '

But he did not get any further, for Colonel Brevington had spurred his horse forward and shouted: 'Hold your tongue, boy, and give way to your betters. You McAllister?'

Wild Bill said: 'No, sir, my name's Hickok.'

'I wasn't addressing you, sir. I was addressing your companion.'

McAllister said: 'I'm McAllister. Who're you?' There was something about the man that aroused his ire right off.

'I am Colonel Brevington, commanding the First Volunteers. I understand from your boy here that you are acquainted with the neighbourhood and too well acquainted with the Indians for decency.' When McAllister remained silent, the man went on: 'Well?'

'Well what?'

The colonel bridled.

'Are you or aren't you?'

'I know this area, sure.'

'Then you will guide us to the encampment of the Indians.'

McAllister said: 'Like hell I will.'

'What?' The colonel rose in his stirrups and screamed.

'I said: "You can go to hell." '

The colonel said: 'Hickok, I advise you to advise your friend to be a little more co-operative for his own good.'

Hickok said: 'That sure sounds like a threat to me, colonel. If I could offer a little advice, colonel, I'd say my friend McAllister ain't easily persuaded – not by threats. I would employ a little tack. Yessir, tack.'

The colonel turned in the saddle and bellowed: 'Major Newton, place this man under arrest.'

Now, I do not doubt that in a western novel, the hero would have drawn his gun and defied his enemies, but I do assure you that only a man a little too big for his breeches or a little loose in the head would have drawn a gun in the teeth of two hundred and fifty volunteer cavalrymen. Even Hickok, doughty gunfighter though he might be, sat very still and watched events with some nervousness as the major came forward, plodding through the snow with a half-dozen soldiers behind him.

McAllister, it must be said, did not take his being disarmed by the soldiers in good part. He called the colonel a jumped up son-of-a-bitch and cast some doubt on the legitimacy of his parentage, whereupon one of the volunteers, no doubt through some misguided loyalty to his commanding officer, yanked McAllister from the saddle and dumped him in the snow. This man was a blacksmith in civilian life and had the build and general aspect of a grizzly bear. In his not unnatural rage at his treatment, McAllister took a swing at this man, connected without any noticeable result and received a blow that would have killed a lesser man. After that he seemed, if not willing, at least reconciled to the fact that he would have to do what he was told.

From his saddle, the colonel told him: 'Get back on your horse, McAllister, and behave yourself. I hope that you have now learned that I am the master of the situation. You will now lead us to the Indian encampment.'

'For crissake,' McAllister said, 'how many times do I have to tell you? I do not know where the Indians are at. A short while back they were camped at the south end of this valley. They moved on and the snow covered their tracks.'

The colonel kneed his horse forward until he could stare down into McAllister's face. He said: 'Mister, you will tell me where the Indians are and you will lead me to them. I am not permitted to put you to the torture, but I shall most certainly look the other way while my men take you for a short walk if you do not divulge the truth to me. Do I make myself clear?'

McAllister looked at Wild Bill and Wild Bill looked at McAllister.

'Jim,' McAllister said, 'you and Lige go back to the house. I'll guide these soldier boys.'

Hickok nodded. 'All right by you, colonel? Me and the boy ain't no further use to you'

'All right,' said the colonel. 'Clear out, Hickok. We'll send McAllister back to you when the shooting's over.'

Lige stood looking at McAllister as if he had seen a god stricken by lesser mortals. He had never thought to see McAllister knocked down by a man who would stay in a condition to walk away. He looked at the blacksmith in awe.

McAllister said: 'Go ahead, Lige. I'll be gone a few days maybe.'

'Yessir, boss,' said Lige. He and Hickok rode away down

the straggling column of soldiers, the stud, Caesar, and the travois following behind.

The blacksmith said: 'On your horse, McAllister.'

McAllister put one foot in a stirrup-iron and rested for a moment against the horse. He turned his head and looked at the blacksmith. He said: 'Don't get yourself shot by some Indian in the next few days, feller. I want you alive so I can take your head off your shoulders and kick it around some.'

The blacksmith brought a fist back and the colonel said: 'Stop that.'

The man looked at his commanding officer appealingly and said: 'This bastard is full of shit, colonel. Leave me knock some of it out of him.'

Brevington laughed, a man among men, and said: 'Time enough for that, I daresay. Let's get on now.'

McAllister swung into the saddle.

He thought: If I don't find some goddam Indians, there's going to be no living with these fellows. If I do find some, there's going to be no living with me. He did not think that the next forty-eight hours were going to be very pleasant to live through. He suspected that before too long he was going to wish that he was dead. It was not a new experience for him. However, it was not one that he would ever get used to.

14.

McAllister had been in some tight corners in his life, but he could not remember ever having been in one like this. One good look at Colonel Brevington and he knew that a lot of grief lay ahead of him if he did not come up with the Indians. Maybe just any Indians. Just so long as there were some abergoins for this self-righteous son-of-a-bitch to shoot at.

McAllister, however, as you will have gathered, had no wish to find Indians of any kind. Furthermore, he did not know where to find them even if he had wanted to. The snow had seen to that. Though when he metaphorically looked himself in the eye and faced up to the truth of the matter, had it been in his interest to find Indians, there were other ways of deducing where Indians might be without having plain tracks to follow.

He and the army, with a sergeant and an enthusiastic trooper pointing their guns in his general direction, reached the place where the band of White Bull had been camped and here McAllister halted. This was the spot where he had once built his own cabin and had lived for a space of two years. That being so, he pretty well knew every inch of this end of the valley. If he had been an Indian chief and had wanted to put his band in a comparatively safe place, there was one direction only in which he could go and that was west. There the breaks lay. There a handful of men could lose themselves in no time at all. It was also a place which, if used judiciously, could be defended by a handful of men against an army. Which was the reason why Greg Talbot had lived there. Somewhere there had been a lawman with his name on a warrant. Greg had put himself in a safe place from which escape would have been easy and where he could make a stand if necessary. But old Greg was now beyond fretting about warrants. He would not be fretting about anything any more.

Rage burned in McAllister. His cold hands gripped the saddlehorn and he shut his eyes for a moment.

A voice sounded like a foghorn beside him.

'Well, man, don't sit there dreaming. I have two hundred and fifty men waiting here eagerly for action.'

McAllister opened his eyes and look into those of the colonel.

'This,' he said, 'is where the Indians were camped. Can you see the tracks of where the band went?'

The man shouted furiously: 'You can cut out that insolent tone as soon as you like, McAllister. I have no time for frontier riffraff of your kind. Now, get a grip on yourself and sniff out these savages. It'll go damned hard with you if you fail me.'

McAllister snarled: 'You think I have second sight or

something? How the hell do I know where the Indians went?'

'You talked with them. The nigger boy told me that. You can't fool me they didn't tell you where they were headed. Where's your conscience, man? These bucks are fresh out of battle, their hands are still red from the blood of our gallant soldiers. You owe it to your own kind? Or are you more Indian than white?'

'This band,' said McAllister, 'was made up of folk who were not in the fighting.'

'You can't fool me with that story,' the man said. 'Every goddam redskin we ever met told us that. Bloody scalps hanging from their belts and pleading innocence. I intend to bring them to book, no matter what, so go ahead. Lead us to them or you won't live to see that ranch of yours again, that I promise you.'

McAllister peered closely at the man. He could scarcely believe he had heard the open threat.

He said: 'Are you out of your mind?'

A major rode up and reined in alongside the colonel.

'Colonel,' he said, 'this man here is a man of some repute. I don't think it wise to treat him in this cavalier fashion.'

The colonel made a great show of turning in the saddle to stare at this source of irritation.

'When I want your advice, major,' he said, 'I'll ask for it. While I am in command here, I shall brook no interference from my officers. Do I make myself clear?'

McAllister watched the major's face go purple with rage. He marked the fellow down as a possible ally. Before he was through here, he was going to need one.

He thought: I don't doubt White Bull has gone into the breaks. But you could lose an army in there and I reckon that Indian knows how to lose himself as well as the next man. So I'll lose this man's army in there.

It could prove risky, but anything was better than having this fool charging down on an innocent village.

He said: 'I don't doubt they've gone into the breaks, colonel. But where they are in there is anybody's guess. We could hunt them for a week in there. On top of that, if they want to put up a fight, you could ride clean into an ambush. You could lose this regiment inside a few minutes.'

The colonel grinned a like a fox.

'No Indian,' he said with authority, 'will expect the army in this kind of weather. He won't expect the Volunteers. We'll catch him with his pants down, McAllister, and we'll make good Indians of every last one of them. Men, women and children. They're all poison.'

The major said: 'It is my opinion and that of the other officers, colonel, that we should turn for home. Even if we started back now we would have been out for over one hundred days. There could be serious trouble over this.'

The colonel smiled in a superior way.

'Newton,' he said, 'there's never trouble for a commanding officer who returns after a sweeping victory.'

'Killing a bunch of old men, women and children ain't going to be a hell of a sweeping victory,' McAllister said.

The colonel's only response to this remark was to raise himself in his stirrups and wave his hand above his head. His cry of 'Forward' rang out on the cold air; horses and men once more began their stumbling advance. McAllister turned and looked back at the soldiers as they huddled, pinched-faced, on their horses. They would be walking again pretty soon in the breaks where the drifts would be twenty foot deep. At the moment they looked as if they could not successfully fight a kindergarten, but he knew that if they met Indians they would be soldierly enough for the work demanded of them. He knew that if he were riding with such a troop against a powerful array of Indians, his attitude would have been quite different. His trouble was that he had a mental foot in either camp; he could not help regarding Indians as human beings since he knew so many of them personally. Only if you could generalize as these boys did could you hate a people. He headed into the breaks and, as he did so, he wondered where Dom Lawson was. If he was hanging around here, there was still a chance that he would seek the opportunity to place a bullet in McAllister's head. The thought did not help to cheer McAllister much.

It began to snow again. When he looked back now, the

soldiers had become like wraiths among the falling flakes.

They pushed on for nearly an hour before McAllister halted.

Now was the time when he started his delaying tactics.

The blacksmith demanded: 'What you stopped for?'

McAllister snarled: 'Get your fat colonel up here. I want to talk to him.'

The blacksmith said: 'You talk polite about our officer, bub, or I'll reshape your face for you.'

McAllister said: 'That's only something you can talk about with an army standing behind you.'

Somebody was sounding off with a hacking cough. McAllister saw that it was the major whom the colonel had rebuked in front of McAllister a short while before. In a few minutes, Colonel Brevington fought his way through the snow and demanded to know what the hold-up was.

McAllister said: 'There's a dozen breaks meet here. The Indians could be up any one of them.'

'What makes you think that?'

'They have to be somewhere.'

'Can't you do better than that?'

'That'll have to do for now. If you search them, your men had best be alert or they could walk into an ambush.'

The colonel snapped: 'My men are always alert.' He bawled for the major and the man came, coughing. McAllister thought he was on the edge of being a very sick man. The colonel said: 'We'll camp here, Newton. See to it. Picket the horses. I want four squads of men on foot, each under the command of an officer. Each one will search a break before nightfall. The men will be on the alert at all times in case of attack. Understood? While they are gone, the cooks will prepare a hot meal. Pitch my tent yonder.'

The major nodded miserably and coughed his way towards the men to give the orders.

The colonel turned and looked at McAllister. He said to the sergeant: 'Tie this man up to that tree there. Armed guard on him at all times.'

The sergeants starting bawling their orders. There was little cohesion in the men. They were tired and all they had on their minds were a hot meal and sleep. McAllister heard them grumbling. The blacksmith prodded him with his carbine and told him to get over to the trees. The sergeant produced a length of rawhide rope. McAllister's hands were tied behind his back and he was secured to a tree. All he could do was promise himself that someone one day was going to pay for this.

The snow stopped and the temperature dropped again. McAllister was not the happiest of men. Tied up to this tree, he could freeze to death. He said so to the sergeant and the blacksmith said he would not mourn him too much.

The sergeant asked civilly enough: 'You reckon there's Indians in these hills, McAllister?'

McAllister said: 'Could be. Who knows? But they won't be hostiles. All the Indians I've seen aren't in the fighting.'

The blacksmith said: 'How the hell do you know a thing like that?'

'Because I've talked with them. I speak their language. They're scared the soldiers will attack them. They have very few young men to do any fighting. They've come here so they can be protected by the soldiers at the fort.'

The blacksmith laughed. 'No soldiers ain't going to protect no Indians. Not while the Volunteers is around.'

'I'm liable to freeze to death,' McAllister said. 'How about getting me a blanket or something?'

The sergeant said: 'I don't know about that. Our boys only carry what they need themselves.'

'There's a blanket on my saddle.'

The sergeant said to the blacksmith: 'Rogers, go fetch the man his blanket.'

'Like hell I do,' said Rogers.

'That's an order.'

'You can order till you're blue in the face, but I ain't running this way and that for this Indian-loving son-of-a-bitch.'

The sergeant went and fetched the blanket himself. He draped it around McAllister's shoulders. McAllister said 'Thanks.' He rested his back against the tree and watched the details marching off into the breaks, struggling through the snow, their carbines ready in their hands. Men were busy chopping wood, cooks were lighting fires. McAllister realised that he was hungry. The blacksmith walked to the next tree, sat down with his back against it and filled his pipe. Puffing at it, he looked utterly contented. The sergeant told him: 'Well, I have work to do. You watch the prisoner, Rogers. I hear he's a slippery one.'

The blacksmith said: 'Not slippery enough to dodge a bullet, sarge.'

The search parties did not come back into camp until a short while after dark. They stumbled into the firelight and hugged the heat to them. They had found nothing. They cursed the Indians, they cursed the army and they cursed their commanding officer. It was always so with soldiers. Towards sleep time, somebody thought to bring McAllister some stew to eat. He asked for his hands to be untied, but Rogers refused him. The man who brought the food ladled a few mouthfuls into McAllister, then grew tired of the exercise and threw the remainder away. McAllister laid his head back against the tree and slept. He could sleep anywhere. In times of stress, he preferred to sleep. Before he closed his eyes, he did the best he could to remember exactly where the component parts of the regiment where – the horses here, the colonel's tent there; the officers, the men, the stores. Ocassionally, he opened his eyes during the night. He never did so without finding Rogers, the blacksmith, watching him until he was driven to wonder if the man needed any sleep at all.

The sergeants were bawling the men out of their sleep before first light. Fires were built up and the cooks had the coffee going. It seemed that a great space amid the great expanse of dark and snow was packed with men, horses and fires. If somebody had told him there were a thousand men here, he would have believed them. McAllister, cold, stiff and miserable, wondered what the hell he was going to think up today.

Major Newton came to speak to him. The man looked even more ill than he had the night before. He squatted down for a while as he coughed. When he was through coughing, he wiped his eyes with his gloved hand.

'McAllister,' he said, 'the colonel wants to know if you have dreamed up any ideas about these Indians during the night.'

McAllister said: 'Does the colonel realize you're a sick man, major.'

'He wouldn't notice a thing like that,' the major replied. 'How about an answer to my question?'

McAllister said: 'If I was free and could range around for sign, maybe I would come up with something. As it is you'll have to go ahead searching all the breaks. If they aren't in the breaks, they'll have moved on to higher ground. Up there, the cold'll freeze your balls. off.'

The major looked despairing. He said: 'The colonel will never loose you so you can search, bank on that. Tell the truth now: if we freed you, you wouldn't look for Indians, would you?'

'You bet your sweet life I wouldn't. There's no sense in it. Chances of finding 'em are small. If I find them, I'm flushing out a bunch of innocent folk who can do no harm to anybody. It would be a massacre and you know it.'

'I know it,' said the major. He looked sick and resigned. 'What can I do?'

'Arrest the crazy bastard,' McAllister said without hesitation, 'and take him back in irons.'

The major said: 'You could be accused of inciting to mutiny.'

'Mutiny my ass,' said McAllister. 'It's your plain duty. It's been done before by a man in your position and it'll be done again.'

'You underestimate Brevington, McAllister. He is a powerful man. A fellow that crossed him could be all washed up in the territory.'

McAllister said: 'If he finds and kills these Indians, it'll be him who's washed up. I'm an impartial witness, Newton. Stop him while he's stoppable, man. Right now the men're tired and they've had enough. They'd back you. If we sight Indians, every man-jack of them will be turned into a hero.'

'I know it,' Newton said miserably. 'But, as you say, I'm a sick man. I couldn't carry this through. I don't know how much longer I can sit a horse.'

'All right,' said McAllister, 'my suggestion is, go ahead searching the breaks here. That should occupy the boys till dark.'

The major coughed some more and McAllister thought he was going to choke. Finally, he coughed himself too weak to cough any more and he staggered to his feet, to stand there uncertainly, staring down at McAllister.

'I'm damned sorry about this, McAllister,' he said. 'Believe me.'

'I believe you,' McAllister told him, 'but that don't help me, lying here tied to this goddam tree.'

The major wandered away.

The cold of the night, intense and physically painful, continued on into the daylight hours. Men hugged the fires, great blazing bonfires, and huddled in anything they could wrap around them. They cursed when the sergeants sorted them out to scout for Indians. A bunch of them surrounded an officer, telling him they wanted to go home. Now. Brevington heard them and roared up, telling them they were cowards and traitors. He promised them Indians that day.

'We'll find 'em, lads,' he said. 'We'll find 'em as sure as God made little apples. And we shall wreak our revenge on them. We'll go home with red scalps to show our girls, boys. They'll strike a medal for this campaign, boys. Every last one of you will be remembered as a hero.'

One of the men made a pert remark which was not to the colonel's liking, and was promptly put under arrest. The man said that suited him fine as it would prevent him from hunting goddam Indians. The colonel danced with rage. He gave the order to break camp. It was not good for men to sit around on their butts all day. The whole command would move five miles west.

An hour later, they moved out. McAllister rode with his hands tied to the saddlehorn. A squad of men went in advance to break trail for the horses and the going was pretty firm. The snow held off, but the cold intensified. Men had the brims of their hats tied down over their ears with scarves. Every now and then, finding it too cold to ride, they dismounted and walked, pounding scraps of warmth into themselves with flailing arms. McAllister had his teeth chattering like castanets. When they halted, he was so stiff that he could scarcely get out of the saddle. The blacksmith thought that was pretty damned funny. He found a tree and tied McAllister to it. A steaming cup of hot coffee in his hands, he sat and watched his prisoner. An hour later, the sergeant brought McAllister something hot to drink.

It was towards the tail-end of the afternoon when a patrol brought a stumbling half-blind man into camp.

The blacksmith went to enquire and came back to tell McAllister that they'd found a man lost, his eyesight almost destroyed by the brilliance of the snow.Then the sergeant came up to check on the prisoner and McAllister asked him about the new arrival. The sergeant described him and McAllister knew that Dom Lawson was in camp. It was not the best news that McAllister had ever had.

15.

When the subject of Dom Lawson came up, McAllister had the feeling that he should have been devious, but he was not feeling devious. He was still feeling enraged by his situation.

It was Newton, the sick major, who came to tell McAllister about the wild ravings of the man who had been found wandering the snow, temporarily bereft of his sight.

The major looked troubled and ill when he told McAllister: 'This fellow has a story of being jumped by horse-thieves a few dawns back. They shot his two companions and stole his horses. His place is down near the first break. He says he dare not go back there, because the rustlers may still be there and gunning for him.'

That was when McAllister should have kept his mouth shut, maybe. Or gone ahead very cautiously. But he did not feel cautious. He felt like hitting out and hurting somebody

'He's a goddam liar,' he said. 'I know him. He's been a thief and a killer from way back. I've carried warrants with his name on them in my time. He came north here to steal my best stud horse. Hickok and I caught him at Greg Talbot's place and laid into him. Sure, we killed one of his men and wounded the other. You saw the wounded man when we met you on Black Horse. The real reason for Lawson coming into this country was for the simple reason of killing me. Hickok rode in to warn me.'

'Why should he want to kill you, McAllister?'

'Because he owes me a killing. Now he owes me another. It's a kind of pride with men like him to keep the score even. It may not mean anything to men like you and me, major, but to him it makes sense.'

'Well,' said Newton, 'he's told his story to the colonel and the colonel believes him.'

'I can believe that.'

'There's more. This man says that he knows where the Indians are located.' He paused to let that sink in. It sank in all right, deep. McAllister sat quietly there and contemplated what this could mean. It did not take much contemplation for him to realize that he was on the edge of a massacre.

He said: 'You know just what this means, major?'

Newton coughed for a while and then said: 'Yes, I know what it means. But I know of no way of stopping it. Yes, yes, I know, I could arrest Brevington, but it's very doubtful if I'd get away with it. If I were sure of the men, it would be different. As it is, they've heard that the Indians are somewhere near and they're already talking of a great victory. They're thinking of their return home, the triumphant entry, every damn one of them a hero.'

McAllister had a simple idea. Not much of an idea, but the only one he could come up with. It did not stand much of a chance, but there was nothing else.

'Major,' he said softly, so that the others did not hear, 'you have to get me loose. These Indians have to be warned, so they can move.'

The major had an objection to that.

'I can't do it, McAllister,' he said. 'As much as I want to prevent a massacre, I can't prepare the Indians so they can cut down on these soldiers. I cannot be responsible for the death of a single whiteman.'

'You're going to be responsible for the death of a hundred Indians.'

'When it comes down to it, a man's loyalties are to his own kind.'

'Your loyalties should be to humanity.'

'Not when it comes down to it.'

McAllister tried again.

'I could give you my word,' he said, 'that the Indians won't fight. I can persuade them to cut and run.'

The major waved a hand at the elements—'Nobody can cut and run in this. We both know it. The Indians will have to stand and fight. That means soldiers being shot.'

'For God's sake, man' McAllister said. His voice was rising. The sergeant and the blacksmith were listening intently. 'You can't sit by and see men, women and children slaughtered like cattle.'

'Don't think it's an easy choice.'

'It ain't so goddam easy for me, neither,' McAllister said. 'I was raised with these folk. They're all human beings to me.'

'That's where we differ. They're not to me. I know every soldier here. They're more than names to me. I know their parents, their wives and their sweethearts. I couldn't face their folks knowing that I'd sent them to their deaths.'

'Aw, shit,' said McAllister. 'So this horse-thief comes in here, leads the soldiers to slaughter a bunch of Indians and ends off his little victory by putting a bullet through my head.'

'That's impossible,' the major declared. 'He wouldn't dare, not with you under military guard.'

'Don't try and fool yourself,' McAllister told him. 'This

bastard could kill me if there were guards ten deep around me. He'll ride off, laughing.'

There was nothing more to be said. The major coughed some more and wandered wretchedly away, despairing and indecisive.

The blacksmith said: 'You goddam Indian-lover.' He pondered a while and added: 'I hope that horse-thief plants a slug in your noddle and no mistake.'

McAllister said, calming down a little: 'Be assured, my friend, before he gets a chance to do that, I shall beat your dumb head in.'

The blacksmith came forward to do something about that, but the sergeant drove him back with a few well-chosen obscenities.

There was just one bonus that day. The sergeant relented and freed McAllister's hands long enough for him to eat a fill of hot stew. That helped him to feel a little better. He searched through the crowd of soldiers, but he could not see Lawson. The sergeant said that he was in the colonel's tent with bandages over his eyes. The command's doctor thought that it would not be too long before the man could see again.

'That's too damned soon for me,' McAllister said.

16.

Colonel Brevington dithered at the present camp-site for two days for no apparent reason. The men were not sorry to be no longer pushing their way laboriously through the snow. They cut great stacks of wood from the trees growing on the hillsides above them and the fires were keep going fiercely. Men stayed close to them and roasted luxuriously. In spite of all this, the morale of the men was low and even McAllister, on the outskirts of the camp, could not fail to be aware that the manner of the men towards their NCOs and officers was increasingly insolent and rebellious.

During the first day, Major Newton collapsed. McAllister saw him go down.

He was fairly well liked by the men and several of them hurried to carry him to his tent. Later, the sergeant informed McAllister that the doctor had diagnosed pleurisy. The man needed warmth, rest and good nursing. There were several more cases of pleurisy and pneumonia among the men, the sergeant said.There was more news. Two men had foolishly tried to desert, though how far they would have gotten or where they were headed was anybody's guess. They had been caught and brought back before they had covered more than a few miles. Brevington had them in irons.

'But,' said the sergeant cheerfully, 'pretty soon we'll come up with the Indians, there'll be a fight and the men will cheer up considerably. There's nothing like a good slice of hot action to put the men in the right frame of mind. This man Lawson seems to know where the savages are at. We'll jump them tomorrow easy as kiss your hand.'

McAllister, being tethered far from the nearest fire, nearly froze to death and he started to feel ill himself. He could not help wondering if his own lungs had become infected and that he was starting to go down with pleurisy also. Searching as he was for any chance to alter the conditions of his captivity, he told the sergeant he did not feel well and demanded to see the doctor.

The sergeant, who had not been unkind until now, was not too sympathetic. 'The doc is here for the soldiers, McAllister. Too bad if you ain't up to taw. It's all in the mind, I daresay. A little cold don't hurt a husky feller like you.'

'A husky feller like me dead from his lungs ain't going to do you much good,' McAllister said.

The blacksmith spoke for his sergeant: 'We don't need you, McAllister. Not now. This feller Lawson can guide us to the Indians. It's a cinch. Hand in your chips if you want, it ain't no skin off my nose.'

During the afternoon of the second day of inactivity, McAllister was dozing. The sergeant woke him with a kick in the ribs. McAllister sat up and blinked around to see a small deputation heading towards him. In the lead was the colonel. Behind were several officers and men. Beside him was a familiar figure. This was Dom Lawson and, to all appearances, he had regained his sight.

As he paced towards McAllister, the man had a fixed and ghastly smile on his face. Like a deathly gargoyle, McAllister thought, as if what Lawson had in mind was at that very moment giving him an obscene and almost intolerable pleasure.

Colonel Brevington halted a foot or two from the prisoner.

He said at once: 'Well, we don't need you any more, McAllister. This man here knows where the Indians are to be found. We shall hit them at dawn and all your base plans to save them from retribution will be thwarted. But you needn't go thinking this lets you off the hook. Mr Lawson brings accusations against you for murder and horse-theft. The army intends to hold on to you and to hand you over to civil law for your hanging. I take some pleasure in informing you of this.'

McAllister said: 'It warms a man's heart, colonel, to hear such public-spirited words.'

Lawson kept his wolf's teeth bared.

The colonel said: 'Well, Lawson, all it needs is for you to identify this fellow before witnesses. Go ahead. Is this your man?'

Now Lawson showed that his sight was not perfectly restored to him. He screwed up his eyes and leaned forward to stare into McAllister's face.

'This is him all right,' he said. 'The murdering, thieving bastard.'

'Good,' cried the colonel, 'excellent.'

McAllister kicked Lawson in the crotch.

The man let out a startled yell of pain and staggered back into the arms of the men behind him. They caught and held him as he voiced his pain loudly and repeatedly. The blacksmith rushed forward to strike at McAllister with the butt of his carbine. The prisoner covered his face with his arms as the heavy weapon thudded home. An officer caught hold of the blacksmith's arm and said: 'We'll have none of that. The man's a prisoner.'

'He's a goddam Indian-lover,' the blacksmith roared.

The colonel danced around on his toes, crying: 'You'll suffer for this, McAllister. By God, you'll suffer.'

Lawson was shouting, as he held his private parts, that he would kill McAllister.

When Lawson had been dragged away, protesting and struggling violently to get to the man who had kicked him, the sergeant said to the prisoner: 'That was a dumb thing to do. I never saw a dumber. You're just piling up grief for yourself, feller.'

McAllister, smiling benignly, said: 'Dumb maybe, sergeant, but it sure made me feel better. And if this goddam blacksmith of yours comes close enough, I'll do the same for him.'

Rogers cocked the hammer of his carbine and said: 'Chance'd be a fine thing. You so much as look at me wrong and I'm going to plant lead in your guts.'

Later, when McAllister asked the sergeant if he could be moved nearer to a fire for the night, the man answered: 'Not a chance. We ain't feather-bedding you.'

17.

McAllister was woken by that boot again. It was not yet light and he felt awful. He heard himself coughing and he thought: I sound like the major.

He heard the sergeant say: 'On your feet. We're riding.' The sergeant walked away and the blacksmith took over. He did not use the toe of his boot but his rifle butt, which was just as effective. McAllister climbed slowly to his feet and found that he was so giddy that every fibre of his body demanded that he lie down again. He seemed to be shaking uncontrollably. He had no sooner discovered this than he began to sweat.

A trooper brought him his horse, saddled and bridled, and McAllister climbed laboriously into the saddle. They tied his hands to the saddlehorn again.

The men were going around, killing the fires. Other men were heaving on mule-packs and the mules were complaining. They did not like the snow any more than the men did. Even the voices of the sergeants were subdued, as if their owners were too cold and too tired to put any effort into their shouting. They would liven up soon when they came within shooting distance of the Indians. Indians acted on troops like a tonic. Nothing like fleeing women and children to make life worth living.

McAllister looked at the faces of the boys carrying the rifles and realized how young they were, too young almost to be blamed for anything. They had been reared to hate and fear Indians. As they should, for they were the invaders. And so it went on. Before them, the Sioux were the invaders and before them . . . it went on through time, the invasion and conquering of weaker people. Right and wrong hardly came into it; it was just something that happened. He did not blame anybody. He just wanted to save a hundred brown men, women and children from bloody slaughter. There surely could be nothing wrong in that.

Over his dead body, he thought. This man Brevington would not lead his men down on the Indian remnant – not while there was life in McAllister's body.

How much life was left in his body? He seemed to ache from head to toe. A rasping cough tore at his chest. His very lungs ached within him. He was light-headed. The sweating had stopped now and he trembled with cold. He felt as though his body would never be warm again.

The colonel was in the saddle. 'Forward,' he cried, like a hero in a dime novel. He raised a hand dramatically. A mule brayed appropriately. He called to Lawson, who was now mounted on an army horse, sitting it uncomfortably because of McAllister's well-placed kick. 'Lead on, Lawson. Find us the Indians so we can finish the job.'

In front of Lawson walked the squad who were breaking trail. Their faces looked dark and shrunken with cold in the bright glare of the snow. Shoulders hunched, they moved forward. They looked as much like soldiers as sacks of corn tied in the middle. But they could kill, thought McAllister, they could pump hot lead into the brown bodies and leave death lying blood red in the snow. He clutched at the saddlehorn for support and kicked his horse into a slow walk.

They pushed on into the morning, travelling slowly, stopping now and then when they met an impassable drift of snow. The sergeants bawled for shovels and the men worked up a sweat while the colonel danced on the outskirts of the activity, impatient with the elements and the men. Finally, Lawson called a halt and said that the Indians were no more than an hour's march in front. The colonel gave the order to camp. Only small fires to be lit. Double guard. Now the men began to be transformed. At last they were pretty sure of a fight. The young ones became tense, but they were happier because suddenly they had a purpose. The veterans mocked them, telling them how they would mess their pants and have Indian-fever the first time they had to fire on living flesh and blood. There was no tree near to which McAllister could be tied, so he was dumped on the snow in the open and the blacksmith watched him with a loaded carbine in hand. 'He won't get away from me, sarge,' he said, 'you can bank on that.'

When it came to eating time, the sergeant permitted McAllister's hands to be untied so that he could feed himself. By now, McAllister existed in a cocoon of sick misery. The perpetual coughing had weakened him and all he wanted to do was to lie down and sleep. But he knew that he dared not sleep, not with the Indians so close. If he could reach them and warn them, he must do that; anything just so long as they had the chance to cut and run. Maybe a few of them would survive days out in the snow. He did not know. But they had to have the chance.

He knew that he must make a break before they bound his hands again. When they bound them, they bound them tight with rawhide and there would be no freeing them. The thought that the vital moment was right on top of him daunted his sick mind. He tried to drive his thoughts and make some plan, but his sluggish brain refused to work. He would have to act and follow one act by another until he reached the Indians and gave them the warning.

His opportunity came just after he had insulted the blacksmith. He called him a few choice names picked out of the air and Rogers rose from the ground, placing his tin of stew carefully upright in the snow before he moved. He slowly picked up his rifle and advanced on the prisoner. First, he paused and looked around to see if he was being observed by a superior officer. When he was convinced that he was not, he raised his rifle to bring the butt down on some vulnerable part of his prisoner. McAllister hurled his mess-tin into the man's face and, as he did so, rose, seized Rogers' clothing with both hands and heaved him with all his waning strength towards him. At the same time he drove up and forward with the top of his head. The blacksmith's nose cracked with the sound of a pistol shot. The man staggered away from McAllister and fell on his back. McAllister rose giddily and dropped his knees hard into the fellow's belly. Rogers' eyes started from his head and his tongue came out. He made a sound rather like a deflating balloon. When he tried to rise, every muscle and nerve in his body screamed its refusal. He tried again and, to make sure of him, McAllister hit him hard under the jaw. Rogers groaned and lay still.

Not for McAllister the quick glance around to see if he was observed. He had to go whether he was seen or not. He dived for the nearest horse which stood saddled and ready for a scout not twenty yards away.

As soon as he started to run, McAllister became acutely aware of how sick and weak he was. His legs started to fold under him so that he expected at any second to be on his knees on the hard-packed snow. Before he could do that, however, his feet went out from under him on the polished surface and he went down. He hit the ground so hard that almost every scrap of wind was knocked out of his body. As he floundered helplessly on hands and knees, he heard the first shout of alarm go up. But he had that horse as his goal and every part of his being was concentrated on reaching it.

On his feet, he wavered for a moment, this way and that. Somebody fired a shot and he had reason to bless the fact that the volunteer's standard of marksmanship was not as good as it should have been. The shot missed him by a foot, but it came near enough to the marksman's comrade to make him yell out in alarm. Slipping and sliding, fighting weakly to keep his feet, McAllister struggled on his way.

How long it took him to reach the horse he would never know, but it seemed like an eternity. Finally, he had the line untied from the picket-pin and was hauling himself desperately into the saddle. Another couple of shots which winged their way viciously but ineffectively above his head and he was astride and urging the horse to run.

The animal was reluctant.

When McAllister, with feeble curses and a kick or two in its belly, at last managed to get the animal to jump forward, it was too late. Something thudded into the animal, it shrieked like a human just once and fell to the ground.

McAllister was hurled helplessly from the saddle, all arms and legs, fought to land on his feet and instead stretched his length on the ground. He heard shouts, the pounding feet of running men.

The first face he recognized as he wearily sat up was that of the sergeant who had charge of him.

'You son-of-a-bitch,' said the sergeant.

'Ain't I just,' said McAllister.

The colonel was there, dancing.

'That's a government horse,' he yelled. 'You are the cause of the death of a government horse.'

'If your soldier-boys could goddam well shoot,' McAllister said, 'I'd be dead and the horse would be walking around.'

One man said: 'We can soon remedy that.'

The colonel danced some more and shouted: 'Who had charge of this man? Where is his guard?'

The sergeant went pale and started bawling out for the

blacksmith – 'Rogers, where you at, man? Where the hell's that Rogers gotten to?'

Somebody discovered him walking around in irregular circles, holding his face and groaning. He was led protesting feebly and denying that he had so much as taken his eyes from the prisoner.

'But he got away from you,' shrieked the colonel. 'You cannot deny that he escaped. By God, you shall suffer for this, soldier. A gross dereliction of duty. A crime for which a man should be shot.'

McAllister grinned and said: 'Shooting is too good for him.'

The colonel turned on him savagely. 'You hold your tongue, sir, or by God I'll forget that I'm an officer and a gentleman. Take the prisoner away and see that he is tied up. Tight. He stays tied tight. Two men watch him night and day. Hear? Sergeant, do you hear?'

'Yessir.'

'I shall hold you solely responsible. If he gets free again, I shall have your stripes and you'll see the inside of a guardhouse. This man goes for trial when we get back to civilization.'

'The only man going on trial back in civilization, colonel,' McAllister told him, 'is you. You have violated every code in the book. You have given succour to a known thief and murderer, you have detained a citizen going about his lawful and peaceful business, you have – '

Maybe the colonel can be excused for what he did next. Maybe he cannot. I don't know. Twenty witnesses saw him strike the said civilian in the mouth. Said civilian made a vain effort to strike back, but was seen to fall on his face and lay there. He did not stir. The colonel looked anxious, then he walked away muttering that he hoped the miserable bastard died.

An officer called the doctor who made a careful examination of the prisoner and declared him to be a very sick man. An officer who remains nameless was heard to say that if McAllister died, he for one would report it as murder. Under the circumstances and obeying the orders of the doctor, McAllister was not tied to a tree or anything else that night. In fact, there was not a vestige of an iron or rope on him. They made up a warm bed for him near a fire and a medical orderly attended him. Just the same, the sergeant and two armed men were within easy reach of him all the time and one of the three stayed awake to watch him.

The following day, there was some argument about what should immediately happen to the prisoner. The colonel said that everybody should stay with the column. They were in Indian country and he was responsible for every life there. Wounded, sick and all the rest should remain with the main force. The half-dozen sick were tied on horses or carried in litters. McAllister, more dead than alive, but warmed slightly by a shot of whisky given him by a merciful doctor, was thrown astride his saddle and there he clung, scarcely aware apparently of what was happening to him.

Lawson came to him and said: 'They saved you for me, McAllister, but don't think you're going to get away with it. I'm going to blow your goddam brains out before the day's done.'

McAllister appeared to come alive a little at this.

He looked at Lawson and said: 'It'll have to be in the back, Dom.'

Lawson said: 'Suits me whatever.' He took his place at the head of the column.

The Volunteers moved forward as quietly as they knew how. Bridle chains and anything that could rattle had been muffled or tied down. Talking was forbidden. The colonel announced that if anybody made any sound which would give the presence of the column away to the Indians he would be severely punished. McAllister witnessed it all as though through a veil. His chest pained him as if a tight band of steel had been closed around it. When he coughed it was as if his lungs were being pierced by red-hot needles. He was told to stop coughing unless he wanted to be gagged.

After an hour or so of slow advance, the column halted while Lawson went ahead with several men to scout the Indians. The men waited by their horses with mounting impatience until they returned. Lawson came back to report that the Indians were still where he thought and that they seemed to have mounted no guards. The army would catch them like sitting ducks.

'Good, good, good,' declared the colonel and rode forward for an inspection of the field of action. He quickly returned to deploy his troops.

The Indians apparently were camped on the far side of a frozen creek. The horse herd was amongst timber on rising ground beyond it. Company A would advance due west from here, circle and come through the timber from the west, driving off the horse herd and attacking the village from that direction. McAllister could have told him that he was wasting his time on the Indian horses. At this time of the year they would be far too weak for riding. They would be best ignored. Company B would attack from the south. Company C under the immediate command of the colonel would approach from the north-east, cross the creek and attack from that direction. The Indians would be caught and there would be no escape for them. Companies A and B would hold back until they saw Company C advancing. That would be their signal.

One of the officers said: 'Let me get this right, colonel. Are you telling us that you aim to hit this village without first checking if there's fighting men in it? I mean – maybe there's only old men, women and children in there.'

The colonel turned and stared at the man unbelievingly.

'Can I believe my ears, sir?' he cried. 'Is this one of my officers speaking?'

The man persisted. 'I would have thought that under any rules of warfare you should know what you're killing before you kill it.'

'It's practically mutiny,' the colonel cried. 'You heard me say, sir, that we shall attack that village yonder. Are you questioning my authority?'

'Not your authority, sir, just your correctness of action.'

'You will obey my order, captain,' the colonel said, 'or you shall answer for it.'

The captain said stoutly: 'I shall obey your order, colonel, because that's my plain duty and I don't have any alternative. But it will be you who answer for it, sir. I shall submit my own report to the authorities after this action.'

Colonel Brevington made a disgusted and impatient sound. He waved a hand in dismissal of the captain. 'Every man here today will boast of this to his grandchildren. Stay cool, men, and beat hell out of the red devils.' He gave the order to move out.

The sergeant in charge of McAllister asked rather timidly: 'What about the prisoner, colonel?'

'He stays here.'

'Me and the boys would dearly like a crack at the Indians, sir.'

The colonel relented. 'All right, bring him forward until we sight the village. You will stay back while we make the charge. That will give you the chance of a shot or two.'

The column advanced. Those who were afoot now rose into the saddle, those with pistols drew them and looked to their loading. Carbines were unbooted. The men's tension and excitement rose. They started talking among themselves until their sergeants hissed for them to stay still. Even the horses caught the excitement and started to act up a little. One man said: 'They can smell the blood even before it's drawn.'

McAllister found himself riding behind the colonel and the captain who had taken Major Newton's place as second-in-command. This was the very officer who had questioned Brevington's attack on the village. Once this man looked back and his gaze met McAllister's. They both understood the situation and both of them in their own ways were powerless.

Although McAllister was still fevered, his mind in a general turmoil and his body scarcely strong enough to keep him in the saddle, there was a small corner of his brain which stayed clear, as though in defiance of the laws of nature. It was this part of his brain which was insisting that he do something to prevent the slaughter on which the troops were nearly launched. He looked around desperately, wanting to get his hands on a gun for just one shot, to make a small startling sound which would alarm the camp and the Indians to save themselves while they still could. There seemed not a chance. He could have wept from the agonizing frustration of his situation. He found as they went forward that tension inside him was mounting to an unbearable pitch.

At last they came to a rise in the ground and he was riding up it, leaning forward in the saddle in order to stay there. The horse slipped a little and recovered itself.

When they halted at the top, McAllister's uncertain eyes made out the cluster of hide tents on the far side of the creek, dark against the white snow, here and there a curl of smoke. Beyond was the forested slope and the dark trunks of the trees where the winter-weakened ponies scratched and gnawed for a precarious existence.

The colonel was saying: 'All right, get moving Company A.' The word went back down the line and the first company peeled off from the rest and, under cover of the ridge, rode off into the south. Quickly the sound of their travel across the expanse of snow died away and they moved soundless as ghosts.

The captain spoke up for the last time.

'I must protest again, colonel, at this action. It is not only unwise, it's improper. Worse than that, it is unchristian.'

This was far too much for the colonel to take – the lay preacher in him was caught to the quick. He turned pale and then red with fury. He stood in his stirrups and the leather creaked under the weight, his horse shifted uneasily at the sound of his enraged voice.

'Brigg,' he said, 'this is too much even for a forbearing man such as myself. I relieve you of all responsibility. You no longer hold the rank of captain in this formation. You shall charge the enemy below there as a lowly private.'

Brigg said: 'You do not possess the authority, sir.'

'We shall see, sir,' cried the colonel. 'Oh, we shall see. Now, I have no more time for the trivia of an officer's poor personal discipline. Move out Company B. Look sharp now before we have the savages all over us.'

There was a surge of movement behind McAllister as the company moved out. Soft-voiced orders were given. Hold file now, close up. Goddam you, hold that fool horse in. McAllister became aware that the formerly demoralized but still exhausted troops were now disciplined and ready for action. Their own wishes made them at once obedient to orders. The orders of the sergeants at once took on the snap of men who knew that they would be instantly obeyed.

Now, screamed a voice inside McAllister's head. It's got to be now.

Until that moment, there had been no sign of life among the Indian tipis. Now a man stepped out of one, scratching himself, stretching and yawning. A dog followed him and started sniffing around, catching a scent. Some wild creature had ventured there during the night. The dog became excited. Across the stillness of the snow, McAllister could hear its eager whimper. McAllister thought that the Indian must look up and see the soldiers' shoulders and heads above the skyline. But the man continued, unaware.

Just raise your eyes for a moment. Just look up and see. There's death for you here on the ridge.

The man beat himself with his arms against the cold. Now the flap of another lodge opened and a bent old man stepped out and stood shivering in the cold, not wanting to go on but ordered on by nature. Go back, old man. Go back.

The dog was running along a line of scent, barking joyously now, heading for the creek.

'Oh, that goddam dog,' said a man nearby.

McAllister rode forward for a clearer view and nobody prevented him. The slight movement made him dizzy and he swayed in the saddle. Slowly, he counted the lodges and knew there were more than when he had counted them previously. Two more? Three more? If young men from the fighting had joined White Bull, would they have been able to bring tipis with them? Maybe they had picked up their women and children somewhere before they fled? He prayed to God that White Bull had no young men fresh from battle down there. In the same breath, he prayed that there would be some young men to protect the women and children from the soldiers.

He thought of White Bull asleep down there with his old

wife by his side. Then, incongruously, he thought of himself back at his own house with his own wife, which he did not possess, at his side, while a couple of hundred or more Cheyenne waited to swoop down on them.

Brevington was still giving orders. He had changed his mind. Now he could see that the whole village was within carbine shot of the ridge. He would dismount his men from here and hold the Indians under a steady and firm fire while his flankers moved it. When the mounted attack was under way he and his men would mount and go to their assistance.

Assistance? The word was a mockery. It would be assistance at a slaughter.

Yet, McAllister did not know. Cheyenne were stubborn people. However few fighting men were down there, they would put up a fight. They would run to stand between the soldiers and their women and children. While they could stand, they would stand. They would die preventing the soldiers from reaching their families. Such was the tradition. There could be a lot of white boys killed here today yet.

Traditional Indian defence under attack was flight; they were a hit and run people, fitted for quick attack and counter-attack. If the attack was too heavy then flight was the answer. But there was an exception to that rule. When women and children were concerned, you stood between them and the enemy. That was what warriors were for, that was their ultimate reason for being. McAllister knew well the tenacity and ferocity of Indians under attack in such circumstances. If they were cornered here today, they would fight in desperate pockets of resistance. Then the colonel would suffer his casualties. Brevington now knew that his surprise was to be total. He saw the Indians surrendering and his men cutting them down. Already the man could see his name in newspaper headlines: GREAT VICTORY OVER THE INDIANS.

McAllister turned once more to look at the faces of the waiting soldiers. It must have been the fever in him, for instead of white faces he saw the faces of the young Cheyenne. He knew in that moment that he must not only save the Indians from the soldiers, he must save the soldiers from themselves. McAllister had lived a tough and hard life, he had killed men without a qualm, but he had never lowered himself to do what was planned here today and nobody's son should be subjected to being forced into such an act. This man Brevington would lead and the young men would follow. He had to stop them committing a crime for which they could never be forgiven.

With a loud shout, McAllister lashed his horse forward.

In that crazy moment there was a sudden and piercingly clear realization that in that single act he had altered a whole situation. Up to that moment, he had not really feared the young white soldiers in any real way. He was the same as them. A whiteman. Now, urging his horse down that snow-thick slope, he had put himself on the opposite side. Suddenly, every rifle there behind him was held by an enemy.

He found that he was shouting in Cheyenne at the top of his voice – 'Soldiers . . . soldiers . . . '

He watched the young man stop, head jerked up, staring unbelievingly. A flap opened and a man's head and shoulders appeared from a tipi. The stooped old man stopped in his tracks, mouth agape.

Move . . . for God's sake, move . . . run for your lives. Listen to what I'm telling you. Save yourselves.

'Soldiers . . . soldiers . . . '

His horse was halfway down the slope, going down in a great shower of snow, front legs stiff, rump sliding. McAllister continued yelling. Now the Indians must see the soldiers behind him. They must see . . .

The flat sound of a rifle shot sang mournfully across the valley. The colonel's voice was raised in a shrill shout – 'Shoot that man!'

There was a stutter of shots. Now the Indians must know for sure. Why weren't they moving? Why did none of them appear from the lodges?

The frozen creek lay in front of him. His horse balked and danced.

Suddenly, Indians seemed to erupt from everywhere.

There were many more Indians than he thought possible. Dark figures darting from the tents, running, hesitating, startled.

From behind him, he heard the strident cry of 'Attack! Attack! Attack!'

Riders were starting to pour over the rim of the ridge. He could see White Bull now, standing and shouting to his people. At once some figures started to run back between the lodges, heading for the timbered slope behind the village. Other figures began to detach themselves and run forward to meet the soldiers. One here and another there dropped to one knee and raised a rifle to shoulder. The blossom of dark smoke came.

He got his horse on to the frozen surface of the creek and the animal slid and slipped across it. It reached the far bank and started up it, floundering a little in the drift of snow there.

As he topped the bank, something violent beyond all possibility snatched the horse from under him as if the animal weighed no moe than a handful of paper. McAllister landed on top of the bank and started rolling and sliding back towards the creek.

When he looked up, the soldiers were on top of him, negotiating the creek and heaving up on to the flat on the far side. One man lashed at him with a sabre, another fired almost point-blank at him and missed. Then they were past him and pounding on towards the village.

There came a ragged burst of firing and when he crawled to the top of the bank, he saw that the cavalrymen had been stopped and were turning away on either hand. Then he heard a cheer and looked to the right and saw the other company of men coming slowly across the snow from the north-east. Brevington's men were turning back, unable to face the withering fire of the Indians. He looked further up the timbered slope and saw women and children struggling to reach the cover of the trees. Then he looked to his left and saw the third company of troops coming in a slow charge. They had seen the refugees and were making for them. There was a white boy sitting in the snow near him, looking ghastly and holding his belly with both hands. He said: 'Oh, Jesus,' and slowly lay down.

The Indians had spotted the charge from the south-east and to counter its approach they drew back among the tipis. No more than a half-dozen Indian rifles were turned on the newcomers. Just the same, their fire was fierce and broke up the charge.

McAllister's legs gave way and he sat down in the snow. He had never felt more frustrated and ineffectual in his life. Now he raised his eyes and saw the Stars and Strips rippling in the breeze above the tents.

He could hear Brevington's voice somewhere, rallying the men. Slowly, the horsemen began to rally. The Indians fired into the mass of riders and two saddles were emptied. Now the Indians drew back again and the bulk of them started to withdraw up the slope beyond, firing and running, firing and running. Firing came from a spot to the right of the camp and, looking that way, McAllister saw that there were Indians there in the mouth of a gully. They seemed cut off by the charge of the second company. The soldiers turned towards this gully, dismounted and lay down to shoot into it. McAllister guessed that some women had taken refuge there and warriors had been forced to make their stand there. They, he decided, were as good as dead. One or two soldiers were riding wide of the gully mouth and were climbing their horses on the ground above from which they could shoot down on to the Indians below.

The soldiers immediately in front of him were riding forward and getting among the tipis. Some dismounted there and began setting fire to them. They found an Indian in one and dragged him out by his hair. McAllister could see that he was wounded and limped badly on one leg. He broke away from his captors and made a feeble run of it. They shot him with several bullets before he had covered a half-dozen paces.

The company from the south was now among the trees. He thought he heard the screams of the women.

There was a man wandering his way through the snow. As he came close, McAllister saw that he was little more than a boy. He wove as he walked, clutching at one arm.

McAllister said: 'What happened, son?'

The boy stopped and stared. He was in deep shock. He walked a few more paces and sat down beside McAllister.

'It's my arm,' he said. 'It's broken, I guess.'

The boy's name was Seth Roberts. He was the son of a dry-goods merchant. While the sounds of the battle came across the snow, McAllister tended the wounded boy, talking him back into the ordinary world. While the boy watched him in a kind of dazed bewilderment, McAllister pulled his coats off and examined the arm. Roberts had had the ill-luck to be hit by two bullets with the result that the arm was horribly shattered. There was no setting this one. The rapidity with which the boy was losing blood was dangerous. By the time the doctor arrived on the scene, McAllister had staunched the blood and covered the wounds.

The doctor, a youngish man with a peppery manner, said: 'He couldn't save your arm, son. But he saved your life.'

When the boy realized that the arm would have to come off, he started to weep. This, McAllister had to remind himself, was one of the kids who had rushed forward in the charge to kill Indians.

He wandered off towards the fight. Now he saw that the warriors had retired up the slope into the trees and there could be seen digging in. The cavalry were hovering among the trees, but all of them had now given up the idea that the Indians could be finished in another charge. On the slope itself, Brevington, sabre in one hand and revolver in the other, was urging his men on towards the enemy. Most of them were laid down in the snow shooting up at the people above them.

There were several dead bodies among the burning tipis. One, McAllister found, belonged to a man of mixed Cheyenne and white descent, a noted trader. He had three bullets in him. On the southern edge of the village, he found a lodge which had not yet been damaged by fire. Inside, he found two people, one dead and one no more than half-alive. The dead man looked to be a halfbreed. With a shock, McAllister recognized him as Sammy Samson, the interpreter. The other man was Captain William Steiner, the Indian agent.

My God, McAllister thought, this puts the cat among the pigeons.

The agent had been hit in the hip by a bullet and another had grazed his skull. The latter wound looked worse than it was, as head wounds always do. He had lost a lot of blood. The bullet to the head had no doubt been the one which had knocked him unconscious.

McAllister tried to pick him up, but in his weak state it was more than he could accomplish. He stopped the bleeding from the head and found some water which he forced between the man's lips. After a while, he opened his eyes.

He recognised McAllister, then at once looked around and said: 'Where's Sammy?'

'Over there, and he's dead, captain.'

The wounded man pursed his lips and said nothing. With McAllister's help, he regained his feet and hobbled outside. McAllister supported him to the doctor who was working on a wounded man halfway between the camp and the creek.

While the doctor was trying to stop the hip wound from bleeding, Steiner said: 'Who's commanding these soldiers?'

'Brevington,' said the doctor.

Steiner said: 'I'll see the bastard hang for this.'

The doctor said: 'If he comes out of it alive. The Indians aren't exactly lying down for him. His officers advised him against it.'

Steiner asked: 'Didn't he see the flag?'

The doctor replied: 'Couldn't miss it. It was just another cunning Indian trick. Maybe he was right at that. You can't deny there's fighting men among this bunch.'

'There's some wounded from a fight, if that's what you mean.' Steiner turned to McAllister. 'Did you lead Brevington here, McAllister?'

'No, I'm a prisoner.'

'What happened to Dick Reynolds, the trader?'

'He's lying dead over yonder.'

'My God,' Steiner said.

McAllister rose, saying: 'I'll be back.'

He walked past the dead trader and came to a young officer lying on his back with his mouth and eyes open. His new Colt revolver lay beside his right hand. McAllister picked it up and searched the body for ammunition. When he had it, he stuffed the ammunition into a pocket and shoved the gun inside his clothing. Now he felt a little better. His recent physical efforts, though slight, had quite exhausted him, so he sat down and took a rest. From where he sat, he had a clear picture of almost the whole battlefield.

The handful of Indians in the gully were still holding out. There were soldiers above them firing down and there was a scattering of troops lying down in a semi-circle on the flat occasionally lobbing a shot into the gully. The replies from the Indians were few and far between, so McAllister assumed there were few Indians left and those who were were short of ammunition.

The Indians among the trees had brought their opposing soldiers to a standstill. They seemed to have good cover among the trees and they had also dug in well at certain points. As McAllister watched, the soldiers tried to rush them, but their shooting was too accurate and the soldiers ran back to their former positions again. The Cheyenne would hold out until dark and then would try to slip away under its cover. How far they would be able to get in this weather was anybody's guess, but, desperately short of warm clothing and food as they must be, they surely could not last more than a few days. The soldiers would walk them down without too much trouble at all.

So what did he do now? he asked himself and he was damned if he knew the answer. But he had to do something. No commanding general in the land would be able to defend what Brevington had done here today.

Something soft and warm touched his cheek. Startled, he turned his head and found himself looking into the eye of his own horse. Now, he did not know whether to laugh or cry. He got up and closely inspected the animal, only to find that there was not a mark on it. It was as pleased as a dog to find him. McAllister patted it on the neck, then climbed into the saddle. There he had another fit of agonized coughing before he went on. The canelo took him back across the creek and up on the ridge. Here he found a handful of soldiers, most of them sick men. Major Newton lay in his litter. McAllister approached him and told him exactly what was happening on the far side of the ridge. He told Newton of the two halfbreeds shot in the shooting.

'There's going to be hell to pay, major. It ought to be stopped before any more lives are uselessly thrown away. Brevington can't avoid a court-martial when he gets back. Steiner's evidence alone will see to that.'

'Except that Brevington probably pulls more weight than Steiner who is largely discredited. The local commander, Major Whitehouse, ignores him and says he's an Indian-lover.'

'There's you and me, we count for something.'

'That man Lawson accuses you of being a horse-thief.'

'Lawson's own record will look after that.'

Shortly after this, the stretcher-bearers started to bring the wounded in. They were laid out on the snow in two rows, more than a dozen of them. The orderlies said that there were as many out there dead. The doctor sweated in the cold.

18.

Hindsight is easy enough. It is the implement of fools. At one time or another, we all employ it. We can look back on a battle, any human incident for that matter, and think that we could have done better than the man controlling it. The battle could have been tidier, the men used to greater advantage, the terrain employed better. But reality is untidy and any human incident is as complicated as the number of participants.

The battle fought at Dead Indian Creek was a mess from start to finish. But one must be just and admit that most of such battles (if they can be glorified by such a name) are the same. Men did foolish things, brave things and cowardly things. Some were cruel, some were merciful and the most unexpected men come out best. And all the time unaccountable things happen.

For example, the laws of nature being what they are, the Indians there should have been over-run and probably killed within the first hour. They were out-numbered and out-gunned. The soldiers had every advantage. But the fact remains that the Indians were still holding them off when dark came.

'One night out in the open,' Colonel Brevington opined, 'and they will come in begging for food and shelter.' It gave him a kind of glowing satisfaction to think that, while he was snug and warm in his blankets, the savages were out there exposed to the elements, the kids crying, the women bewailing their fate, the bucks wishing that they had not defied the soldiers. Dawn would reveal them to be abject. The lay-preacher's prayers were rapturous that night. He knew that the Lord was smiling on him.

Little did he know that the heavens were full of divine laughter. His God mocked him. Those who were on high were being cast down. Even as he prayed and gave thanks for the great privilege of his victory, the Indians were quietly picking their way north through the winter trees, clutching their threadbare blankets about them, some of them even half-naked in the cold, and slipping out of his grasp. The children were hushed and all was silent as the remnant of a band slipped away to freedom and possible death.

While they were doing this, the soldiers ate and smoked at their blazing fires, totally surrounding the savages. No one, they thought, could slip through such a tight cordon. When dawn came, the colonel's rage was something to be seen. He stood and gazed at the footprints in the snow, the only concrete evidence that the wretched Indians had ever been there. He raged. He would have the balls of the men who permitted this to happen, captains would be broken to the ranks, sergeants would be punished. Could he trust nobody? Must he bear the whole brunt of this campaign himself? Was he the only man in the whole miserable regiment who possessed a sense of duty?

He roared for the men to saddle their horses and follow

those same footprints through the snow. Ride the dogs down. Sabre them to death. Turn the snow red with their life-blood.

The divine laugh sounded again. As the men went to their horses on the picket line and saddled them, so the soft and inoffensive flakes came fluttering down from the heavens and, as they watched, so the footprints slowly vanished before their eyes.

'I don't believe it,' cried the stricken colonel. 'I just do not believe it.'

He lost his presence of mind then and ordered small parties of riders out to search for the Indians. Old hands told him that they would lose themselves, but he would not listen to advice. He had to have those damned Indians. Not a single one of them should live. His victory must be total.

By night, of six parties which went out, four only had returned. One would never return, for they had the misfortune to be successful. They had found some Indians. Three young Sioux, all wounded, and a handful of Cheyenne women and children, huddled and hiding. The Indians, their women aiding them, had attacked the soldiers with sticks and bare hands, having lost their weapons in the surprise attack. The three soldiers had died and the Indians had gone on.

The other party came in the following day, frost-bitten and sick. They had lost a horse down a ravine and two of the men were riding double. They all had the shocked and frozen look of men who were surprised to still be alive.

Captain Harry Brigg had a noisy scene with the colonel which was witnessed by practically the whole regiment. He demanded that the regiment now turn back and return to base. Rations were low and the men were at their last gasp.

The colonel shouted: 'You have no authority here, sir. I broke you on the scene of battle.'

Brigg said: 'I am still an officer of the volunteers and I must warn you that if you do not from here on act reasonably, I shall be forced to place you under arrest and escort you home under an armed guard.'

Once more the colonel had howled 'Mutiny'. but no one

failed to notice that he did nothing about it. He retired in a profound sulk to his tent and stayed there while Brigg assumed command.

Brigg's first anxiety was for the scouting party of four soldiers which was still missing. The pressing need was for him to get his men to some source of food supply before the rations ran out entirely, but he could not bring himself to move on without the missing men. Thinking that Dom Lawson knew the area, he asked the man if he would lead a search party, but Lawson flatly refused. However, McAllister volunteered. The doctor said that McAllister was not fit to ride. For all he knew, he said, McAllister had pneumonia on top of the pleurisy. But McAllister insisted. It was now Lawson's turn and he vigorously opposed McAllister's going.

'The man's a thief and a killer,' Lawson said. 'Can't you see? He's trying to get away from me.'

McAllister said: 'I wouldn't get away if I was offered gold. I'm staying to see that Brevington answers for his work here.'

Captain Brigg said: 'I believe you.' He assigned an experienced sergeant to McAllister and detailed five men to accompany them. He added: 'And you don't have all the time in the world. This is the last day of half-rations. Tomorrow we're down to a quarter.'

McAllister led his party into the north-west. They wandered for two days until they rode down on the men lying dead under several inches of snow. It was a miracle that they found them at all. When they had buried them in the hard ground and said a few good words over them, they turned back. By this time, the fever had reached its height in McAllister and he was at once ordered rest and warmth by the doctor. He lay with the other sick and wounded near the fires and privately the doctor told Brigg that the man was as good as dead.

'How he made that ride, I'll never know,' he said.

However, McAllister's iron constitution had been assailed before and survived. And it survived this time. The fever broke in the night and he started to mend. He was, however, too weak to sit a horse and so was placed in a litter on the side of a mule. He slept almost solidly for three days. When he finally came to himself and felt more or less back to normal, he was informed that the regiment was once again lost. He stepped down from his litter and mounted a horse, pale and shaky.

He led them the following day through the gateway of the fort and there gave its commanding officer brevet-Colonel Robert Whitehouse the poser of his career. Makeshift quarters were found for the men and the cooks worked overtime to dish up some good hot food. Whitehouse wrung his hands, despairing of continuing to feed so many men.

'My God,' he said, 'I've scarcely enough supplies for the garrison. How the hell do you think I can feed a whole goddam army?' He made some fairly wild talk about the incompetence of amateur volunteers and stated that nothing of this kind could have happened if there had been a professional officer in charge.

The scene took place in his office. It was here that Brigg informed him that he had placed his own colonel under arrest. It should have been comparatively simple thereon, but Whitehouse chose to make it something else.

Present there were Whitehouse, Brigg, Lieutenant James Lawrence now acting as second-in-command to Brigg with the volunteers, Steiner the Indian agent and McAllister. The last was present because Steiner had requested him to be there and because of the friendship and understanding which had grown up during the march between McAllister and Captain Brigg. Colonel Brevington still sulked and was sitting in his borrowed quarters dividing his time between praying and drinking. Major Newton was still a sick man and was confined to quarters on the doctor's orders.

When Whitehouse demanded to know why Captain Brigg had arrested his colonel, the captain replied that his superior had behaved irrationally.

'Irrationally,' said Whitehouse, 'in what way?'

Brigg replied: 'His behaviour was irrational. These gentlemen will agree with me, I'm sure.'

Whitehouse snapped: 'Ten men may agree with you,

captain, but that does not make it so.' Any captain who could arrest so august a rank as a colonel was suspect in the major's book. He was, after all, himself a self-appointed colonel. 'Tell me just how irrational.'

'He insisted on attacking an Indian village without first ascertaining if it was hostile.'

Whitehouse sat up sharply with interest.

'Where was this village located?' he demanded.

'On Dead Horse Creek.'

'Dead Horse, did you say?'

'Yes, sir.'

'Go on.'

'I and the second-in-command, Major Newton –'

'Is that the officer under arrest for mutiny?'

The captain said: 'The officer lying sick —'

The fort commander said: 'This is beginning to sound very like a conspiracy to me.'

'If you'd allow me to finish, sir.' Whitehouse gestured for him to continue. 'We both begged him to reconsider and to check the village before we attacked. For all we knew there were only old men, women and children there.'

'Were you aware, captain,' the man behind the desk asked icily, 'that we were at war with the Indians?'

'I was aware, sir, that we were at war with the Sioux and Cheyenne and then only with certain of their bands. We had no way of knowing what tribe these people belonged to.'

Whitehouse said: 'It might interest you to know that, with the climate and mood of the nation as it is now, I would have done the same as Colonel Brevington. Our orders are to attack and destroy the Indians wherever they may be found.'

'I am sure that can't mean that we have to make war on women and children. I'm sure our men did not volunteer for that kind of service.'

'Don't you be too damned sure.'

'And there is one more thing, sir.'

'What?'

'The Indian camp was flying the Stars and Stripes.'

Whitehouse barked off a laugh. 'Any villain can shelter under a flag. You're gullible, captain.'

Captain Brigg was getting mad. He got to his feet and he raised his voice a little. 'I'll have you know, sir, that flag was given to the Indians by Captain Steiner on the sincere understanding that the Indians would be safe under it.'

'Steiner!' Whitehouse snorted. 'We all know he's soft on Indians, don't we?'

Steiner said: 'It may also interest you to know, colonel, that I was in that camp when it was attacked. I am a witness to all that went on that day.'

'What?'

Whitehouse was shaken now. For one moment, he was at a total loss for words.

'I had not understood . . . '

Steiner said: 'If you'll listen for a while, colonel, you'll understand considerably. I was in that camp and Sammy Samson was with me. Sammy would also be a witness, but he was killed by army bullets. The trader, Reynolds, was also in camp. The soldiers shot him as he tried to run towards them telling them not to shoot. Now Sammy and Reynolds were both well-known figures on the frontier. You're not going to write those two off with a careless laugh. Brevington's going to answer for this. You're not going to settle this here and now nor are you going to brush it under the carpet. Newton, Brigg and I are army men to our bones and we have the good name of the service at heart. We're not going to be stopped by anybody.'

Now Whitehouse turned hard.

'I'm not at all sure that your accusations are valid, captain,' he said. 'So far as I have understood matters both Newton and yourself have been deprived of rank.'

'Added to which the colonel is under arrest,' said Brigg.

McAllister said: 'You're forgetting me, colonel. Remember, I came to you and asked for protection for White Bull's camp? There's your refusal to answer for. And there's something else.'

'Such as?' Some of the snap had gone out of Whitehouse's voice.

'The fact that I am laying charges of false arrest and murder against Brevington.'

Now the colonel wanted to be rid of them all. He washed his hands of the whole affair, he said.

'I want you all out my fort,' he said. 'I do not have the rations here. It's always the same with these volunteer regiments. They always bite off more than they can chew. More trouble than they're damn well worth.'

19.

Outside the office on the edge of the parade ground, a bitter wind blew from the north. Captain Brigg and McAllister stood with their backs to it. Brigg had to cup his hand near McAllister's ear to prevent the wind from carrying away his words.

'Can I rely on you to come back to the capital with us, McAllister?' he asked.

'You couldn't stop me,' was the reply. 'Brevington will be making charges against me and I shall be making charges against him.'

The captain slapped McAllister on the back and they parted company. McAllister crossed the parade ground in the direction of the barrack room which he shared with fifty or so soldiers. When he reached the doorway of the barracks, there was a man leaning there, smoking a cigarette. As he came close, he saw that it was Dom Lawson. He stopped and eyed the man. Lawson smiled, showing his wolf teeth.

'Feeling safe now, Rem?' he asked.

'I never feel safe when my back's turned to you, Dom.'

'Nor you should, old friend. Nor you should.' He pushed himself upright, as if he was ready to go on his way now that he had seen McAllister. 'I was just checking up on where you were sleeping. I like to know where you're at all the time, Mack.'

McAllister said: 'You're going to hang around me just one

minute too long one day, Dom. Then you'll look up and see there's a rope around your neck.'

Lawsom laughed genuinely, his eyes dancing with an unholy delight.

'There's always the old-fashioned solution before we get to the rope stage.'

'What's that? A bullet in the back?'

'Right first time. Which gives me a distinct advantage, don't it? I mean you wouldn't ever do that to a man, Rem old-timer. You're too goddam fancy for that.'

'A shot from the front is always a possibility, Dom,' McAllister reminded him. 'Don't forget that.'

Lawson said: 'I don't have no scares about that. I could always out-draw you, Rem. You're good with a gun, but you're slow.'

McAllister stood silent for a moment, then he said with an almost whispered menace: 'You're tempting me, Dom. If I can't win with a gun, it might be a laugh to break your neck right here and now.'

Lawson's eyes became uneasy.

'Not here,' he said. 'Not on a military post.'

'What have I got to lose?' said McAllister. He stepped back a half-pace for a blow and saw the uneasiness in the man's eyes become fear.

'Jesus,' Lawson said, 'you touch me and I'll kill you.'

McAllister said: 'You're going to kill me any road, remember?'

Maybe McAllister never intended to strike him. Certainly Lawson's next move prompted instinctive action. As the man tried to duck away, his hand darted quick as a striking snake's head into his open buffalo coat.

McAllister caught at the tail of the coat and swung the man with all his strength, which was still not considerable. Lawson was almost torn from his feet. He turned like a clumsy dancer and his face seemed to bounce off the log wall behind him. As he came away McAllister laid the flat of his hand across the man's face and knocked him from his feet. Just the same the gun came out. It appeared just as McAllister stamped down with a boot-heel into the man's belly. Lawson went a sickly green colour and started to retch. McAllister took the gun from his hand and hurled it over the building.

Very slowly, Lawson came to his feet. His eyes were venomous.

He went to say something, but McAllister's words cut his off – 'If you're going to kill me, Lawson, you'd best do it soon, because I'm going to nail your hide to the barn door. You stole your last horse for a while. I've not forgotten Greg Talbot.'

'Who the hell's Greg Talbot?'

'He's the old man you killed and threw out into the snow like a piece of garbage. He was a friend of mine.'

McAllister turned and walked into the barrack room. He felt good. He had not felt so good in a long time. He walked down the long barrack room to the far end and found a large and powerful man sitting on his bunk. It was Rogers, the blacksmith. McAllister halted and two eyed each other. The blacksmith's eyes were mocking. They challenged McAllister to do something about him.

McAllister took a short inventory of his own emotions and found that he still felt good.

'I see,' he said, 'that you've come for the whipping I promised you.'

The man nodded.

'That's about the size of it,' he said.

'Maybe I don't want to fight,' McAllister said. 'It might make things look bad for me. I mean – there's the investigation and the court-martial coming up. I have to be a little careful. Maybe we should postpone it. If it's all the same to you.'

'It ain't all the same to me,' said the blacksmith. 'I promised myself I'd beat your head in and I have a notion to do it and right this minute.'

There was a good deal of interest on the part of the soldiers. They stopped whatever they were doing and edged nearer for a ringside seat.

McAllister said: 'You boys're going to be disappointed. I don't have any reason to fight this man.'

A corporal said: 'He told me you was yellow, McAllister.'

'He did?' said McAllister with an intelligent show of interest.

'He sure did,' said the man. 'He said you had a yellow streak a foot wide clean down your back. He saw it when you was running away from them Indians.'

'Is that a fact?' said McAllister. 'Maybe you'd like to creep into the fight now. You look the kind of sneaky son-of-a-bitch who gets in after the fight starts and you know who's going to win.'

The corporal said: 'Why, you – '

McAllister's left hand shot out quicker than the eye could follow, catching the corporal in the throat. The man would have fallen backwards on the nearest bunk, but he was prevented by McAllister's hand, which caught his clothing and whirled him off his feet. It seemed that, when he was in mid-air, McAllister hit him again. The man then changed his direction and landed on the chest of the blacksmith, just as that worthy was rising to his feet to hurl himself on McAllister.

As Rogers lay pressed against the bunk by the weight of the corporal on top of him, he felt his ankles seized and, as he threw the corporal from him, he was whisked off the bunk and dumped bodily on the floor. His dismay was utter when he heard his own breath sigh helplessly out of him. If there was any scrap of it left, that was further forced from his lungs by McAllister ramming his boot down on his solar plexus, precisely as he had done with Lawson. Why employ a new tactic when the old ones still work?

By this time, a third soldier had already declared himself in support of his two comrades and was charging down on McAllister. The big man turned just in time to duck under a thrown fist and then dodge a kick for the groin. Without thinking his right hand caught at the ankle and yanked the man from his feet. This put him on top of the blacksmith who was struggling, not very successfully, to rise. The result was satisfyingly chaotic. The corporal, climbing off the bunk, trod on Rogers' face – which was no laughing matter when you remember that the corporal had not yet removed his heavy cavalry boots in preparation for bed. The blacksmith swore rather obscenely and the corporal took his foot from Rogers' face and placed it on his sore belly. Rogers struck out blindly and knocked the corporal's legs from under him. As he went down, his head struck first the side of the bunk and then the floor. So far as he was concerned, the fight was over. As for the blacksmith, he came up on to all fours and from that position launched an attack which was as slow as a drunken buffalo's. All McAllister had to do to finish him was ball his fist and slam him behind the ear. Rogers subsided peacefully on the floor.

The other soldier, who had so quixotically but foolishly entered the fight, leaned weakly against the side of the bunk and said: 'Jesus – you're a goddam Indian.'

McAllister said: 'Ain't I just.'

He was saved any further embarrassment socially after the fight by a breathless runner who came to tell McAllister that Colonel Brevington wanted to see him immediately.

As the corporal and the blacksmith rose groggily to their feet and looked about them unbelievingly, McAllister said: 'I shan't report this cowardly attack on a defenceless civilian, men. I shall put it down to delayed battle shock. Tidy my bunk and we'll say no more about it.' They watched him turn and walk down the barrack room.

If Colonel Brevington had any reason to be embarrassed to face McAllister, he showed it not. He employed the same abrasive and abrupt manner that he had shown all along. McAllister found him in a small storeroom which had been cleared for him to use as his quarters while in the fort. A truckle bed had been provided but little else. The colonel sat on the bed and, not wishing to sit beside the colonel, McAllister chose to stand.

Brevington lit a large cigar, gaining a lot of smoke and not much pleasure from it.

'Well, McAllister,' he said, 'you've gotten yourself into one hell of a fix, man, and no mistake.' When McAllister said nothing, the colonel shifted his feet and tried again. 'You should not have refused to guide me to the Indians, you know. That was real foolish of you. Do you not agree?'

He cocked his head on one side and looked at McAllister almost coquettishly.

McAllister said: 'Get to it, colonel.'

'I am willing to let bygones be bygones,' Brevington said. 'By that I mean I have obtained the victory which the army so badly needed. The Indians were utterly routed. Defeated. We cut them down in their scores.'

McAllister said: 'I was there, colonel. I saw how many went down. And there was plenty got away. You also lost a whole lot of men yourself, colonel. Too many for the army to give you a pat on the head.'

The colonel pointed at McAllister. So far he had managed to remain comparatively calm. 'Now you see here, McAllister . . . be still and hear me. For your own good. I'm not a man who bears a grudge. I am not a malicious man. I'm a soldier and a man of God. Possible to be both, you know. I fight and I pray hard. As a real two-fisted, red-blooded man should. Agreed? Right. So how do we stand?'

'I charge you with murder and wrongful arrest, said McAllister.

'I don't think you heard me,' said the colonel.

'Every goddam sickening word I heard,' said McAllister.

'Now let's talk about this sensibly like men,' said the colonel.

'How about Steiner and Newton and Brigg – have you talked to them sensibly like men?'

'They're soldiers,' said the colonel with incredible confidence. 'They lost their heads in the heat of battle. Green hands get like that under fire. Went through that kind of thing myself years back. They'll come around and show themselves amenable to discipline. I know. There's just you, McAllister. You're the only bad apple in the basket, as you might say. I'm trying to save you a whole lot of grief, man, can't you see it? I carry a hell of a lot of weight in the capital. The governor's a personal friend of mine, the commanding general is a cousin of mine. I'm a power in the community. What hope do you think you have, boy? You don't have a prayer. I tell you that for nothing.'

'The charge is still murder, Brevington. You shot Sammy Samson and you shot Indians who were sheltering under a flag you should show some respect for.'

The colonel was on his feet in a second, face enflamed and eyes wild.

'Now you have gone too far, sir. I will have not one foul word said against my relationship with the flag. The emblem of our nation which I hold sacred.

McAllister felt like throwing up.

He said: 'Murder, Brevington.'

The colonel quietened suddenly.

'What does a man have to do,' he said softly through his clenched teeth, 'to get to you, McAllister?'

'You could try admitting you're a murderous bladder of lard.'

The vein in Brevington's forehead swelled. His fists clenched. Then slowly he subsided. He was slowly getting to the point he wanted to reach.

'I'm trying to get something into your thick skull,' he said.

'Such as?'

'How to make you show some sense and face up to the realities of the world.' There was almost a pleading note in Brevington's voice. Here was a man trying desperately to be understood.

'Well,' said McAllister with a charming smile, 'you start off with a bribe.'

The colonel looked at him like a man who was not too sure whether he was being mocked or not. 'How much?' he asked gently.

'Whatever my price is,' McAllister told him, 'and whatever it's made up of, you don't have the right kind of thing and if you did there wouldn't be enough of it.'

'You're making a grave mistake,' Brevington said. 'I'm making you an offer in a civilized way. Use your sense and take it.'

McAllister said: 'I should have known better than to come,' and headed for the door.

With sudden urgency, the colonel said: 'Wait.'

McAllister stopped and turned at the door.

Brevington said: 'There are more ways than one of stopping a man.'

McAllister considered him gravely for a moment and then said: 'Now you're talking my kind of language, Brevington. Now we get to the threat. There's a bullet somewhere out there waiting for me. You won't hold the gun nor fire the shot. Your kind never do. There's Dom Lawson all ready and willing. You sanctimonious bastard, you'd use a cut-throat and a horse-thief to do a job you're too damned scared to do yourself.' He opened the door and added as an afterthought: 'I hope you know the number of men who've tried it before. Just bear this in mind: when I've killed Lawson, I shall come looking for you. You'd best be hidden or a long ways off. If you had any sense, you'd run now because pretty soon nobody in this territory is going to want to know you.'

He left the room then and slammed the door behind him. Brevington stayed very still and said to himself over and over again: 'I'll kill you, I'll kill you, I'll kill you.'

20.

Dom Lawson was shaking with rage when McAllister left him to stride into the barrack room. The horse-thief at once ran around the building and started searching in the snow for the gun McAllister had hurled over the building. The light was beginning to go now. The snow on this far side of the building was at least two feet deep. It took the man a good ten minutes to find the weapon. When finally he retrieved it, he realized that he had no more than half-heard the scrimmage which had taken place in the barrack room. He put this down to some horse-play among the soldiers.

As soon as the Colt gun was in his hands, he dried it as best he could with his bandanna, emptying out the loads and knocking off the percussion caps. Drying the chambers was a tedious chore and it took time in the poor light which rapidly turned to full dark. He worked on by the dim lamplight that came from the windows of the building. Then he had to reload. He found that his hands were shaking, partly from cold and partly from his fury which had not subsided. He hated anybody to touch him. To have hands laid on him violently was more than he could bear.

He knew that he was going to kill a man. He knew that he did not care how many witnesses there were to the act.

Now he hurried back along the side of the building and turned the corner to the door. As the barrack room came into his view, he saw a tall figure walking down the length of it towards him. Hastily, he ducked back out of sight. He watched McAllister leave the building and head at an angle across the parade ground. Lawson know that he was going to see Brevington. That damn fool Brevington, he should know that a man like McAllister could not be persuaded by words. He could not be persuaded by anything, not even a bullet. He had to be stopped. And Lawson, under Brevington's protection, was the man to stop him. Lawson knew that, if McAllister had to be stopped by force, Brevington wanted the shooting to take place at the right time and under the right circumstances. Such thoughts were quite foreign to the gunman. If you wanted a man killed, you shot him and that was the end of it. You took your chance on whether you answered to the law for the crime or not.

Lawson's rage still rode him. So he stayed near the barrack building and watched Brevington's door. He was very cold and he put on his heavy gloves so that his right hand might be warm enough to handle the gun.

He waited until his patience began to wear thin and the simple idea of going into Brevington's quarters and shooting McAllister down seemed good. He started across the open space and walked into the cold north wind. For a moment, it almost stopped him in his tracks. Its cold blast penetrated his clothing and seemed to cut through his flesh to the very bone.

He was halfway across the parade ground when the door to Brevington's room opened and the silhouette of a large man appeared black against the lamplight within. Lawson knew this was the best target he would have offered to him tonight. Hastily, he shucked the glove on his right hand and reached the gun out from his belt inside the buffalo coat. The butt was ice-cold to his grip.

As he lined the gun up for the careful shot, McAllister stepped forward and slammed the door behind him. With the sudden cutting off of the lamplight, Lawson lost sight of him completely for a moment. For that moment, he debated if he should put the gun away and wait for a better opportunity. As he did so, he glimpsed McAllister, or so he thought, against the lamplight of a window. Lawson turned himself slightly and fired.

He heard the crash and tinkle of glass. His target cried out in a shrill alarm and Lawson knew that he had fired at the wrong man. He turned, trying to probe the semi-darkness with his sight.

He saw the muzzle-flash before he heard the dull report of the big revolver. A bullet whined past his ear, alamingly close. But he was not a man who lost his nerve under fire. He knew that the muzzle-flash was the best target he might be offered that night. He fired two shots and knew as he did so that the man he aimed at had rolled and was now shooting from a another position. It came to Lawson with an undeniable clarity that he would never win while he was standing out here in the open, most likely a clear target against the white snow. So he did what was the only thing a sensible man in his position could do – he turned and ran. McAllister fired two more shots and then there was silence except for some cries of alarm on the far side of the parade ground as the shots came near some unfortunate soldiers standing there.

Lawson stopped running when men began to pour from the buildings. Sergeants were shouting. Who was the goddam fool who'd been shooting? It must be Indians, somebody suggested. Indians had broken into the fort. Colonel Whitehouse appeared on the scene. Lawson blended with the crowd, and stayed there until the hubbub died down. Then he strolled across to Brevington's quarters. He found the colonel very agitated and drinking whisky to steady his nerves.

As soon as he entered, Brevington demanded: 'Was that you doing that shooting?' Lawson admitted that it was and the colonel said: 'You damn fool. I had not yet decided that McAllister had to be killed.'

Lawson said: 'I make my own decisions. I decided long ago that I was going to rub McAllister out.'

Brevington nodded. 'I have made my decision now. McAllister is not to be dissuaded from his ill-advised action. He will have to be killed. But we won't have you going off half-cock again, Lawson. Next time, we'll be organized. Done with the greatest precision and economy. One bullet, one dead man.'

Lawson showed his wolf-teeth.

'My pleasure,' he said.

21.

The journey on from the fort was one of the most curious experiences of McAllister's career. It was as if, for a while at least, all the differences in the regiment, indeed between the colonel, Lawson and McAllister, had never existed. It seemed to be tacitly agreed that all that mattered for the moment was to get the soldiers safely home and that alone was going to take all the officers who could be mustered. Even Newton, still pale from his sick-bed, was determined to do his bit. As though nothing had happened he assumed the position of second-in-command under Colonel Brevington. The colonel himself was rather subdued, but apart from that he seemed near his normal ebullient self. True, he did not socialize with his officers, but he did not bully them either, which was in itself something to be thankful for.

Sledges had been constructed for the carrying of supplies, and the mounts of the dead soldiers were employed to drag them. It was a slow and hard ride which they undertook and it covered the best part of a week, but it was carried out in a disciplined and soldierly manner. There was less complaining now than there had been on the outward march.

'A fine body of men,' Colonel Brevington declared, 'I'm proud to command them.' McAllister could have believed that he was living through a fantasy to see the man's behaviour and his ignoring the fact that he had been arrested by one of his own officers.

Before leaving the fort, Steiner, Brigg, Newton and McAllister had held a council of war and Steiner, though still a sick man, had shown his determination to ride with the regiment to the capital. Indeed Major Newton had begged him to do so.

'Without you,' the major said, 'we hardly have a case. The fact that you put that flag up over the Indians' camp and it was you who was shot by the soldiers makes our case unanswerable.'

So Steiner went along. To McAllister it seemed that there was enough going against Brevington to finish him for life. He was therefore all the more amazed by the calm with which the man seemed to face his future. Maybe that was to be explained by the presence of Dom Lawson at his side. In fact, Lawson seemed never away from his side. He rode there, quiet as a cat and as smug as one with a bowl of cream at its disposal. His official position was that of army scout. He had found the Indians, and he had led the soldiers to them, hadn't he? Now and then, McAllister would catch the man watching him.

There was a band and a large crowd to greet them when they slowly rode into town. It was not exactly a triumphal entry, but it was not an ashamed one either. Every man there was glad to be alive and their folks were glad to see them alive. It was all very curious and McAllister was fascinated by it all, finding it almost impossible to believe that he had been made a prisoner by the army and that he had witnessed the attack on the village.

There was Colonel Brevington having his hand shaken by everybody who could get near him. McAllister watched him join his wife in a coach. She was a happy-faced woman with rosy cheeks and six children. Brevington beamed and beamed. Steiner remarked to McAllister: 'I have to remind myself that that's the man who threw Sammy Samson out of church and who was the cause of Sammy being killed.'

Newton was embraced by a lovely young wife who bore him away to their home on the outskirts of the city. Captain Brigg and McAllister found themselves rooms at the Williamson Hotel which, they found, offered them first-rate accommodation and excellent food. If there was trouble ahead, McAllister made up his mind to enjoy the fleshpots till trouble arrived.

Newton and Steiner were not slow off the mark. The first thing they did was to hire a smart lawyer, a young fellow not long out of Chicago and eager to win fame and fortune for himself. Which was the way McAllister liked lawyers to be. He spent more than a day in Steiner's room taking dispositions from them and asking a lot of questions. That done, he went away and studied his subject. When he came back and had dinner with them one evening, he said: 'Gentlemen, I think we have a good case.'

Steiner smiled at that and said: 'By God, you better had or we're all washed up.'

McAllister was arrested at two in the morning. The city marshal came with two heavily-armed deputies and marched him to the city jail. There was nothing personal about it; they were merely three men doing their duty. They were polite and they did not rough him up at all. One of them, Henry Mackie, he had served with as a policeman in Wichita, Kansas, some years before. In reply to McAllister's question he said that Newton and Steiner had been placed under house arrest. McAllister was a little surprised that Steiner came under military jurisdiction and the marshal said that was most likely because Steiner was on the reserved list of officers. What were they accused of? Newton for disobedience to an order in the face of the enemy. Steiner with consorting with the enemy. What about Brigg? He had been informed that charges were pending.

McAllister went into his cell, knowing that he was there because Brevington was pretty confident of himself. He wondered what he had up his sleeve. He found himself in a neat, clean cell.

He told Mackie who turned the key in the grill door: 'You run a nice place here, Henry.'

'Glad you like it,' said Henry, 'there ain't too damn many who say that.' They laughed a little.

McAllister made himself comfortable on the cot provided and did his best to catch up on his sleep. He looked forward to breakfast and hoped it was as good as the service here indicated. Emergenceies always made him hungry.

But he never got to eat breakfast. At seven in the morning, Henry Mackie came and unlocked the cell.

He said: 'My God, you must have influence, Rem. Somebody got the justice of the peace out of bed and put up bail for you. A thousand dollars. How about that?'

McAllister was puzzled. 'I don't know anybody who owns a thousand dollars,' he said.

He walked into the marshal's office and to his amazement found James Hickok there, smiling widely.

The marshal said: 'This has to be a historic occasion, boys. Rem McAllister bailed out by Wild Bill Hickok.'

Hickok and McAllister shook hands and McAllister said he had never been more pleased to see anybody. The marshal handed him his gun and he strapped it on. He shrugged himself into his heavy coat and he and Hickok walked out on to the street. They braced themselves against the blast of cold and headed for McAllister's hotel.

'Where the hell did you get the thousand, Jim?' he asked.

'Sat up all night playing cards,' was the reply.

'We won't discuss whether it was a straight game.'

Hickok looked prim. 'No, you're right, we won't.'

They talked as they walked. Apparently Hickok had trailed McAllister soon after he and Lige had reached McAllister's place. He had a nasty feeling in his bones that Brevington could not be trusted with a prisoner.

'You stretched friendship just as far as it'll go, I reckon,'

McAllister said and that was the only way he could adequately express his thanks.

'I never heard of any limit,' Hickok replied.

When they were in the warmth of McAllister's room, they peeled off their coats and Hickok produced a bottle of whisky from a pocket. They agreed their stomachs were empty and it was the wrong time of day for strong liquor and then both put a healthy ration of the fiery liquid down them.

Hickok said: 'Rem, I've been talking with that Steiner. He's a nice guy. He's in a real fix himself, but he shows a hell of a concern about the fix you got yourself into. He's told me the whole story. I have a notion you trusted him and you'd told him the whole story from your point of view.'

'Yes. Steiner's straight. Did he tell you about Lawson trying to kill me back at the fort?'

'Sure.'

'Him and Brevington are tied in together tight.'

'That's the way my thinking's been going. Lawson's the long stop. If all else fails, Lawson kills you. You still insisting on the charge of murder against Brevington?'

'You bet your sweet life. The man's a murderer, so it's only right. I've seen good men hanged for less than he did.'

'So now I have you out on bail, Lawson will have to do something about it. I don't know if the marshal's office is straight here, but I can't help suspecting that you would never walk out of that cell into a courtroom.'

'Yet the marshal let me go without a protest.'

'What else could he do?' Hickok added: 'I reckon you would of been found hanging by the neck in that cell.'

'So unless I keep my eyes open, I'm liable to be arrested for something else on the street and put back in the cell again.'

'Most likely. If not, Lawson has to cut down on you. I suspect that when Brevington hears about you being out on bail, he'll lose a little nerve and that'll be the time to set you up. Which ain't going to be as easy as all that with me watching your back.'

'Jim, how can I begin to thank – ?'

'You can buy me a damn good breakfast. I ain't eaten in a coon's age.'

McAllister laughed and headed for the door. 'Just so long as we both eat with our backs to the wall.'

'Sounds like sense to me,' said Hickok. 'I got to confess it's a habit with me after all these years.'

22.

It was twenty-four hours later. They had gathered in Steiner's room at the hotel. Since McAllister's leaving the jail, nothing had happened. And there is no greater a strain for waiting men than the happening of nothing. Even McAllister and Hickok felt it. Now Hickok had gone out on to the icy streets while the others quietly took a drink together and talked. It was evening and the lamps were lit.

When Hickok came in he was frozen and said he would tell them nothing until he had a decent drink under his belt. They gave it to him, he peeled off coats and scarves and held the floor. It was patent to all of them that he was enjoying himself hugely. McAllister thought that this might be meat and drink to the famous gunfighter, but he was damned if he enjoyed one single minute of it. He suspected that the pleasure on Hickok's face indicated that lead would soon be flying and McAllister, being a sensible man, was not over-fond of flying lead.

They all urged Hickok to get it off his chest.

'Well, gents,' he said, 'it has been a good evening's work, though I says it myself as shouldn't. I'll spill all the beans so that you may examine them. First, I have been courting a young hired girl in Colonel Brevington's establishment, which, I may say, was no hardship on my part. I was ever partial to members of the fair sex. Happily, this young person has showed some profound affection for yours truly and has shown a propensity to do all that I ask of her – in the nicest possible way, of course. Now, it so happens that she has been used by our enemies, among others, to spy on our movements and take intelligence of our plans to Brevington and so to Lawson. If all is well, she will relay to her employer McAllister's next movements so that he may put his plan of murder into action.' Hickok beamed around on McAllister as if he had done him the best favour in the world.

'Thank you for nothing,' McAllister snarled with genuine displeasure.

Hickok raised a magnanimous hand – 'Wait, my friend. All will come well in the end. Just bear with Uncle Jim. I have in my possession the exact information we need to nail this Lawson in short order . . . . and in the act of murder, so that, when we gets his deserts, it will be an act of self-defence on our part.'

'Get on, for God's sake,' McAllister said, 'don't make such a song and dance about it.'

Hockok's smile of self-congratulation did not leave his face.

'Rem is anxious to get at the enemy,' he cried. 'It was ever thus. How I like to see keenness in a man!'

'Jim,' McAllister said with some menace in his voice, 'if you don't – '

'Very well, here's the long and the short of it. Lawson will take up his position at an angle to this building on the far side of the street in the mouth of the alley there. When McAllister comes out of the main entrance of this hotel, Lawson will fire. Now, we all know that he is a superb shot. It is his opinion and mine also that he will need no more than one shot, even with a revolver.'

'This gets better and better,' McAllister muttered blackly. 'I suppose he has a cover gun somewhere.'

'That's true. Bright of you to guess.'

'There had to be the way this is stacking up against me. Who is the cover gun?'

Hickok hesitated and pulled his nose, a habit of his when he was attacked by indecision.

'Ah,' he said, 'there's the rub.'

'You mean you don't know?'

'That's what I mean.'

'Marvellous,' said McAllister.

'May I continue?'

'I never learnt of any way of shutting you up.'

Hickok went on: 'But we're prepared, Rem. To be forewarned is to be forearmed.' He smiled amiably. 'I shall be behind you. A long way behind you, but there just the same.'

McAllister looked uneasy and asked: 'When does all this happen?'

Hickok took his watch from a vest pocket, glanced at it and said: 'In about fifteen minutes. I hope your gun is cleaned and ready.'

McAllister stood up and asked: 'Do you know what Lawson will be wearing?'

'No.'

'What's the light like on the far side of the street at the mouth of the alley?'

'Not good.'

'But I shall be in the light when I come out of the hotel?'

'That's right.'

McAllister gave his friend a bitter look and said: 'You sure you're on my side?'

Hickok grinned. 'Brevington tried to bribe me, but he couldn't meet my price.'

'What was that,' said McAllister, 'five dollars?'

Steiner asked. 'We know what you two will be doing, so what do the rest of us do?'

McAllister and Hickok glanced at each other. Hickok gave an almost imperceptible shake of his head and McAllister said: 'Soldiering and such, we leave to you, gentlemen. This kind of thing is also for professionals. In this case, that means Jim and me.'

Steiner said: 'But we must do something, man. I can hear from what you say that you don't like this at all.'

McAllister nodded. 'Jim expects it. If I welcomed his plan, he'd think there was something seriously wrong with me.'

Newton said: 'Why not just go into hiding? Avoid the shooting.'

'Because,' said McAllister, 'I have been through this kind of thing before. We have a smart enough lawyer, but they have more money so they get them a smarter lawyer. He'd worm them out of this. These men are villains. Let's catch them flat-footed in the middle of a crime so that law and order can see it all happening. What is cleaner and juster than me defending my life?'

Newton said: 'Still and all, I don't think this is really the correct way to do it. This kind of thing should be settled in court.'

McAllister said: 'Maybe you're right. I wouldn't argue about it. But if all turns out well, you for one will not have to go into the witness box and testify and answer a lot of questions which will get folks to believe all sorts of bad things about you. Thrown mud always sticks.'

'That's true,' said Newton. 'I can't deny it. But what am I to feel if you get shot down?'

Hickok said briskly: 'We don't allow that kind of talk before a fight, major. Bad luck. Rem's going to come through this. You'll see. Him and me've seen all this before. A good many times. You just stand at that window there and watch it all. Maybe you'll be watching a little bit of history.'

McAllister and Hickok heaved on their buffalo coats. They were some kind of protection, for they could deflect an angling bullet. McAllister buttoned his, then checked the loads of his gun. It was loaded in every chamber, a thing unusual with him, for he normally kept the hammer on an empty one for safety. He then dropped the gun into his pocket. The others watched him. He put his hands into his pockets so that he had his hand on the gun.

Hickok left his coat open and also the jacket beneath. His two Colt revolvers he wore over his pants, high and with butts forward. This made some men think that he used the cross-draw, but he did not. He used the reverse draw, a movement which seemed awkward and, to some, almost impossible, but it was his natural way of drawing and he did so with unequalled speed.

McAllister said: 'Now, let's get this straight, Jim. Lawson will be taking up his position just around now?'

Hickok checked his watch again and said: 'Right.'

McAllister sat down and produced his pipe. When he had

filled it with his rank, black tobacco, he fired it, saying: 'It's cold out there. We can't make Lawson sweat, but by God, we can make him freeze.'

Hickok looked delighted. Steiner offered McAllister another drink, but it was refused. McAllister looked calmer as the minutes ticked by. When he had smoked his pipe out, he looked positively tranquil. He rose, put on his hat and said: 'Ready, Jim.' The others wished him luck, he thanked them and walked out of the room. Hickok followed him. When they reached the foot of the stairs, Hickok stopped his friend with a touch on the arm–'Give me time to go out the rear door, Rem, then to reach the street. Count twenty, say, and don't hurry it.'

McAllister told him to go ahead. Hickok walked to the rear of the hotel and let himself out into a small yard there. This yard opened on to a narrow alleyway. Ten paces along this and Hickok was on the street. He peeked out and saw the dark maw of the alley in which by now Lawson should be stationed. He experienced the small flutter of doubt and panic that comes to all men who have lived by firearms and tense moments such as this. He prayed that everything would go right. After all, he thought, his friend's life depended on it. That girl could be playing him false and he knew it. She may have set this up on instructions from her employer. Suddenly, in an awful moment of truth, Hickok was convinced that that was what had happened. He had been too damned smart for his own good. For McAllister's own good. Suddenly, desperately, he wanted to call it off.

Then he saw Brevington.

There were a good many people abroad in spite of the intense cold. The saloons and dancehalls were doing a roaring trade. Many miners were in from the hills with their summer's gold and were living it up to their own loss and the profit of the townsfolk. Among the hurrying figures on the sidewalk was one solid one that had halted. His hat was pulled down so the lamps cast a heavy shadow over his face, but Hickok, who never forgot a shape, the way a man had of standing, knew that it was Brevington. Hickok could not believe that the colonel intended to be Lawson's cover man.

He was the kind of man who hired for his dirty work to be done.

But Brevington's presence there showed Hickok one thing–the process was now too late to stop. He pulled back the heavy skirt of his buffalo coat. The opening of his clothes let the cold blast in so the sweat on his body froze. He was startled by it into full wakefulness. He took a half-pace forward and hoped that he was not revealed too much in the lamplight. From his new position, he could see the front of the hotel. He could not see the windows enough to make out the watching men there, but nobody could have stepped from the front entrance and been missed.

Brevington had not moved. He stood about thirty paces to Hickok's right. The gunfighter reckoned that the man must be able to see him, Hickok, plain and clear. But Hickok dare not change his position because he wanted the mouth of Lawson's alley in his view. Just the same, he would have preferred to be behind Brevington.

Now an appalling thought came to him. What if the girl had not given him all the information? Maybe she did not have it all to give. Maybe there was a third or fourth man on this street, ready to cut down on McAllister. Hickok cursed his own and McAllister's vanity for thinking that only their kind could settle this kind of affair. They should have let the soldiers play their part. They knew weapons and they were used to being shot at. Brigg would have been a useful man to have along.

He glanced up and down the street and saw nobody who might be an assassin, except for every other man there. Dread for McAllister sank like cold clay into the pit of Hickok's stomach.

He glanced back at the hotel entrance and found that a tall, dark figure stood there. McAllister – hand in pocket, still as a rock, back straight. Hickok's right hand touched the ivory-plated butt of his gun. He glanced right and saw Brevington move.

By God, the man was going to take a hand. That was a sawed-off shotgun he held.

Where else?

A window on the far side of the road suddenly opened and the lamplight caught at something there. A rifle. Hickok drew both guns. He knew then that this was going to be a massacre. Brevington had at least one hired gun here.

While Hickok's nerves were tensed for a gunshot from one of three men, he was startled when it came from a fourth. McAllister pulled his Remington from his overcoat pocket and fired.

The manner in which he fired so surprised Hickok that for a second he held his own fire. McAllister fired high and his action seemed madness itself, for it must have been several feet above the head of the concealed assassin.

There was, however, method in McAllister's madness–a fact of which Hickok should have been aware.

The bullet struck a sloping roof that came down sharply to the top of the fence bordering the alley. The impact of the big bullet moved the snow there and it came down in a great deluge.

Now suddenly Hickok's hopes and spirits were up. He saw McAllister firing up at the window across the road from him and heard the bullet crash through the glass. Then McAllister had hit the pavement with his left shoulder in a long fast dive. One shot sounded from the alleyway. Hickok looked right and saw the shotgun levelled. He fired twice and the greener went off with a deafening roar. Men were shouting in alarm.

McAllister was rolling. The man in the upstairs window leaned out for a clear shot and Hickok drove two bullets into him. He stayed leaning out of the window.

Brevington was down, but the twin-eyes of the shotgun were turned in McAllister's direction. Hickok fired, did not stop to see if he had made a hit and swung back for the alley mouth. He saw Lawson run out into the open to make sure of his shot. McAllister and he seemed to fire in the same second. Hickok fired twice from each gun and all four bullets ploughed into the gunman. They hurled him back against the wall of the building behind him and dropped him to the sidewalk.

Hickok stayed where he was for a second, blowing the

acrid smoke away from him. He put his right-hand gun away, but retained the left. There was one shot in it and he might need it yet.

Brevington lay with his head resting on an outstretched arm.

Hickok looked down the street and knew a kind of disbelief when he saw that McAllister lay still. It did not seem possible to Hickok that McAllister could be proved to be mortal.

'Jesus,' he said to himself, 'I don't believe this.' But he knew that he had to believe it. This was something that came to all gunfighters sooner or later.

He walked down the street and found himself joined by three other men, all with guns in their hands. He saw that they were the men they had left in Steiner's room.

Steiner said: 'We came to take a hand, but you were too damned quick for us.'

They reached McAllister and Hickok said in a kind of hushed voice: 'Rem, old-timer.'

McAllister opened his eyes and said conversationally: 'Well, that's that, gents.'

Hickok said with great bitterness: 'You son-of-a-bitch, I thought you was plumb killed dead.'

McAllister sat up. Then he stood up. He looked a little embarrassed.

He said: 'It was like this, Jim–I just could not believe that I was alive. My God, I didn't ought to be.'

'That's a fact,' said Hickok.

There was a lot of the sounds of running feet, shouting. The law arrived on the scene. The law arrived too quickly for Hickok's liking, in fact, and later he reckoned that one of the lawmen was another backup gun for Lawson. Never could prove anything, of course.

Brevington, they found, was alive. He appeared to go out of circulation in town from then on. That did not mean that he died of gunshot wounds or anything like that. Just that he thought it better to change his name and start afresh somewhere else.

Lawson and the unknown gun up at the window were both

found to be dead. McAllister said that he sadly regretted not having killed a man who had stolen his best stud horse himself.

The questions followed. They stood on the freezing street and had the marshal and his deputies firing questions at them, which McAllister reckoned were a sight better than bullets. Finally, the undertaker came for the dead and the marshal told them they could go, but were not to leave town. The five men walked back into the hotel. When they were in the warmth of Steiner's room and each man held a glass in his hand, the Indian agent said: 'Well, maybe you ironed out our problem here, boys, but I can't help wondering how old White Bull and his folks made out in the hills.'

McAllister said: 'Indians die in the cold just like white folks, that's for sure.'

'Well,' said Hickok, 'I reckon a man has enough to be thankful for, just being alive.'

'That's a fact,' said McAllister. 'Let's drink to Wild Bill Hickok.'

'Aw, shucks,' said Jim.